THE LONGEST STRIDE

THE LONGEST STRIDE

...Branimir stepped closer to Austin, their elbows brushing as he leaned against the wall to look at the mare. "If she learns to trust humans again, she would make an excellent brood mare. Her name's Mary's Gospel. She's been trained for the track, but she never really took to it. Billings got her cheap when her last owner decided to get rid of her. Mary's one of the most talented jumpers I've seen and she used to have the courage for cross-country, if you were thinking about eventing with her."

"You seem to know a lot about her," Austin observed with a raised eyebrow.

"I've been trying to buy her from Billings since he bought her. I knew he'd ruin her given half a chance. Why do people keep giving that man horses to train? He's managed to mess up every one he gets, unless they were already psychotic when they moved into his barn." Branimir shook his head and backed away. "I've got to get going, but like I said, when she's healthy again, if you want help regaining her trust, give me a call."

"I'll do that."

They shook hands, and Austin watched Branimir stroll out of the barn. Okay, so maybe he ogled the guy's ass, presented in faded jeans tight enough to make Austin's mouth water. Everything in Austin shouted not to let Branimir walk away, yet there wasn't any reason to keep the man around. Where had he heard the name Branimir Javlosk? It wasn't the usual run-of-the-mill name. He snorted, and Mary's Gospel startled at the noise.

Austin wandered off to find Carlos, his head groom. They needed to work on putting weight on Mary's Gospel before he worried about anything else...

THE LONGEST STRIDE

BY

T. A. CHASE

AMBER QUILL PRESS, LLC
http://www.amberquill.com

THE LONGEST STRIDE
AN AMBER QUILL PRESS BOOK

Amber Quill Press, LLC
http://www.amberquill.com

Copyright © 2012 by T. A. Chase
ISBN 978-1-61124-926-2
Cover Art © 2012 Trace Edward Zaber

PUBLISHED IN THE UNITED STATES OF AMERICA

To my readers, I hope you enjoy a different kind of shifter.

PROLOGUE

Branimir Javlosk stood in the brisk fresh air of a Kentucky night and stretched. It was time to change. He could feel the need rippling under his skin. As he allowed his shift to come over him, he closed his eyes.

The moment the change ended, he opened his eyes. Snorting, he nodded his head up and down, while shaking all over. He neighed, calling out to all the horses in the area. The other stallions called back, but he didn't have the urge to go and challenge them. They had their own herds, and he wasn't interested in stealing any mares from them.

He reared, kicking his legs to the moon, before taking off down one of the trails in the woods bordering his horse farm. He ran up and down the paths, leaping over fallen trees and splashing through puddles. Branimir loved the freedom being a horse gave him. He slowly let his animal take over and he allowed his sorrow to be pushed back into his sleeping human brain.

The moon was setting when Branimir returned to the hill overlooking the barns on his farm. He shifted back and lay on the ground, staring up at the stars. Searching out the brightest one, he smiled.

"I miss you, Til. I know you didn't want to leave, and it was like getting my heart torn out when I realized what happened to you. It's been five years since you've been gone and I'm beginning to see the end of the darkness. Maybe this year will be the year I fall in love again." Branimir sighed and pressed his hand against his chest to feel his heart beat.

"I have so much love left in me and I know you wouldn't want me to stay alone the rest of my life. You were my first love, Til. The man who taught me what it was like to trust someone and to believe in someone. You shared so much with me, yet I kept the very core of myself away from you, and I'm sorry for that."

Branimir was sorry. He'd loved Til with every atom of his soul, but he'd learned to keep secrets. Too many other lives counted on him not telling anyone. He chuckled and grinned.

"You'd have freaked out, but thought it was cool."

He stood up and dressed before heading back down to his empty house. Til's death had left a hole in his heart and a cold spot in his bed. As he opened the door to step into the kitchen, a gentle breeze brushed over his cheek, and his heart settled. Somehow, it felt like Til gave him his blessing to move on with his life and keep their dream of their horse farm going.

CHAPTER 1

"God damn stupid bitch."

Austin spun around as the loud yell echoed over the clapping of the crowd and mingled with the squeals of an angry horse. He raced through the wandering people, trying to find out where it came from. He'd never turn his back on an animal in distress, especially a horse.

Pushing through a traffic jam of horrified gawkers, he spied a tall man holding the reins of a thin, trembling mare in a rigid grip. He beat her around her head, and when he couldn't reach it with his whip, he hit her shoulders and chest. The chestnut mare squealed in terror and anger, but she couldn't get away from the man.

After pulling out his phone and tossing it at a nearby groom, he shouted, "Call the police."

There wasn't a thought in his head except to get the horse as far away from the man as possible. He looked at a couple of riders who had joined the edge of the group. They nodded and followed him. Austin grabbed the reins, while the other two tackled the man.

"What the fuck? Get off me. What the fuck do you assholes think you're doing?"

The man kicked and swung punches, but his captors got him away from the mare before taking him to the ground. One yanked the whip from his hand and tossed it away. The other pinned the man's arms with his knees and placed his hand around the abuser's neck.

"We're stopping you from hurting that horse anymore. I should've said something the minute I saw you arrive yesterday, Billings, but my

3

optimistic nature got the better of me."

Austin wanted to ask Juan what he meant, but the mare kept rearing and tugging on the reins. She had no idea things were going to get better for her. All she knew was pain, fear, and angry voices shouting. Her nerves were shot, and Austin could tell she was on the verge of a complete breakdown.

"Juan, I'm taking the mare away from here. We'll be in my barn when the police get here."

"Get out of here, AJ. Edward and I've got Billings. We'll talk to the police and find you." Juan waved a hand in Austin's direction, but didn't look away from where he crouched over Billings.

With soft words and no sudden gestures, Austin encouraged the stressed mare to follow him. He never forced her to do his will, knowing it would only lead to another battle. While she was at least five hundred pounds underweight and swaying on her feet, she was still stronger than he was. Unfortunately, he couldn't talk to her and tell her everything would be different now. However, Austin would insure no one ever hurt her again.

By the time he got her to his barn and into a stall, they were both sweating. He got her tack off, tossing the expensive leather into the aisle without a care about ruining it. Billings could go to hell for all Austin cared. He stepped out of the stall, closing the door slowly.

Austin propped his arms up on the top of the stall wall and stared into the well-lit twelve-by-twelve box. The mare trembled, her long legs shaking and her sides heaving. Standing there, wondering when the next hit would come was eating away at her reserves, and he knew, if the vet didn't come soon, the mare would go down. Yet her wild eyes glared at him. Austin swore the glint in them told him she wasn't going to break.

"AJ."

He turned at the softly called sound of his name. He watched Edward Monterrose, Juan Romanos, and a uniformed officer walk toward him. Taking a few steps away from the stall, he held out his hand.

"Thanks, Juan. You, too, Edward. I appreciate you helping out."

Juan shook his hand, while Edward slapped his shoulder.

"No problem, man. We got there at the same time you did, or we'd have put a stop to it sooner." Edward stepped back and gestured to the officer. "This is Officer Masterston. He'll take your statement and get pictures of the mare. Do you think you could get her outside in the sunlight? Also, the vet's on his way over. Those wounds should be treated right away."

"Officer." Austin rubbed the back of his neck as they all looked at the mare in the stall. "I'm not sure if I could get a halter on her now. She's too upset."

Edward snorted. "I'd be upset, too, if I had that jackass Billings as an owner. Poor girl could stand to eat a flatbed of hay as well, I'm sure."

"I think we should just leave her in there. It might be too traumatic for her to have anyone in the stall at the moment." Juan shook his head in frustration. "I knew when I saw Billings arrive yesterday, I should've said something to the officials, but I'd hoped he'd changed his ways after the last time I reported him."

Masterston looked at Juan. "You've reported him before?"

"Yeah. I can give you the name of the officer I talked to about it as well, though it was at a different show out of state." Juan propped his fists on his hips. "I just don't understand how any human can treat a horse like that."

"It's more common than you'd think."

The four of them turned when those words were spoken in a deep, raspy voice. Austin's eyes about popped out of his head as he gazed at the man standing behind them. Everything about the man screamed cowboy, from the black Stetson he wore on his head to the scuffed black boots on his feet. Worn Wrangler jeans and a dark blue T-shirt with a logo on it completed the outfit.

"You are?"

The stranger removed the hat and held out a hand. "I'm Branimir Javlosk. I own Freeland Creek Farm and Rehab Center out of Paris, Kentucky."

Austin shook Branimir's hand, frowning slightly at the familiar name. Why did he know that name? Where had he heard it before?

Branimir's grip was firm, yet gentle. Almost like Austin had always imagined a mother alligator's jaw would be while she ferried her babies to the water from the nest. Enough strength to hurt, but still soft enough to hold a butterfly in his fist without harming it. The random thought of how Branimir's touch would feel on his skin shot through him and stiffened his cock.

Ugh! Totally not the time to be getting a hard-on. Austin shifted as he let go of Branimir's hand.

"Nice to meet you, Mr. Javlosk. I'm Austin Spellsin."

5

Branimir nodded. "I recognize you. I've seen you around the shows. You're a good rider and have some pretty talented horses."

"Thanks." Austin gestured to Juan and Eddie. "This is Juan Romanos, Edward Monterrose, and Officer Masterston."

"Gentlemen, good to meet you all. Have to say this is quite the collection of riders. I saw the incident earlier." Branimir moved closer to the stall, his movements slow and easy. "I came to check on the mare."

"I wouldn't go in there if I were you," Austin warned, but apparently Branimir didn't hear him.

The man spoke softly as he slid open the stall door, yet he made no effort to go inside.

"Do you want to give me the camera? I'll take the pictures from here. I wouldn't want to bring her out at the moment. She's calmed down some, but I'm afraid if we bring her out, she might freak again. No need to stress her out anymore."

Masterston handed Branimir the camera, and he snapped photos of the mare's wounds. He kept up a gentle murmuring, letting the mare know he was there and he wasn't going to hurt her. Austin watched the mare, hoping what they were doing didn't disturb her too much.

She kept her eyes on Branimir, but her stance was relaxed and unconcerned. Austin narrowed his gaze. The mare studied Branimir like a herd animal keeping an eye on her leader. After finishing the pictures, Branimir returned the camera to Masterston and moved farther into the stall.

"Be careful."

Branimir didn't turn away from her, just waved at him. "I'll be okay. Why don't you go talk to the officer? I just want to reassure her. I'll stay until the vet gets done checking her over."

Austin smiled slightly and gathered the others to walk out of the barn. For some reason, he trusted Branimir. A guy who ran a rehab/rescue center for horses wouldn't harm a healthy animal, much less an abused horse.

"Can you describe what you saw? One at a time."

They gave their statements to the officer, and Masterston took their names and numbers while promising to be in touch. They went back inside to see Branimir shutting the stall door before shaking the vet's hand.

"What did he say?" Austin pointed his chin at the retreating vet.

Branimir frowned. "She's five hundred pounds underweight.

6

Another couple of pounds and she'd go down for good. The mare's covered in fresh wounds and has a ton of scars. She'll never win a show based on looks."

Austin leaned on the wall and glanced at the mare. "I don't care. I'm going to see about getting custody of her. She deserves to have a good life after dealing with that bastard Billings."

Branimir growled.

Austin shot the other man a glance. "You know him?"

"Unfortunately. I've gotten a few of his horses into the farm over the past couple of years. For some reason, people keep giving him animals to train and ride. I couldn't get anyone to listen, even with evidence. Do you think they'll be able to get him this time?"

"We've got a ton of eye witnesses, plus the vet's testimony. I think he'll lose all his business and his reputation." Austin sighed. "I guess I'll leave her here for right now and have Sammy give her some food."

"The vet left directions on how to feed her." Branimir dug in his pocket. "Here's my card. Give me a call when you're ready to help her get better. I think I can probably help."

"Really?" Austin took the card and studied it. It had phone numbers, both cell and home.

Branimir smiled. "Not with the physical stuff. That'll just take time and food, but I can help with the mental and emotional stuff. Teach her to trust us again. I don't know if she'll ever be good for anything other than eating her head off in a pasture."

"I don't care about that." Austin frowned. "I just want her healthy and happy. If that means I never ride her, so be it."

The older man studied him. "Do you mean that?"

"Yes. I'm trying not to sound conceited, but I'm sure you recognize my last name." Austin waited until Branimir nodded. "So you know any horse I own doesn't need to perform for me to keep them. I'm not saying my father wouldn't rather she earn her keep, but hell, I run the horse side of the business."

Branimir stepped closer to him, their elbows brushing as he leaned against the wall to look at the mare. "If she learns to trust humans again, she would make an excellent brood mare. Her name's Mary's Gospel. She's been trained for the track, but she never really took to it. Billings got her cheap when her last owner decided to get rid of her. Mary's one of the most talented jumpers I've seen and she used to have the courage for cross-country, if you were thinking about eventing with her."

"You seem to know a lot about her," Austin observed with a raised eyebrow.

"I've been trying to buy her from Billings since he bought her. I knew he'd ruin her given half a chance. Why do people keep giving that man horses to train? He's managed to mess up every one he gets, unless they were already psychotic when they moved into his barn." Branimir shook his head and backed away. "I've got to get going, but like I said, when she's healthy again, if you want help regaining her trust, give me a call."

"I'll do that."

They shook hands, and Austin watched Branimir stroll out of the barn. Okay, so maybe he ogled the guy's ass, presented in faded jeans tight enough to make Austin's mouth water. Everything in Austin shouted not to let Branimir walk away, yet there wasn't any reason to keep the man around. Where had he heard the name Branimir Javlosk? It wasn't the usual run-of-the-mill name. He snorted, and Mary's Gospel startled at the noise.

"Sorry, pretty lady," he murmured, not wanting to upset her even more. "It'll come to me. Until then, you and I are going to work on fattening you up. Things are going to be different from here on out. I wish you could understand me. It would make things go so much easier."

Austin wandered off to find Carlos, his head groom. They needed to work on putting weight on Mary's Gospel before he worried about anything else.

*   *   *

Exhaustion rode Branimir hard, but he managed to make his way to his truck without embarrassing himself by falling on his face. It had taken a lot out of him to convince Mary's Gospel he and the doctor meant her no harm. The mare had been on the brink of a complete collapse, mental and physical. While he did what he could to shore up the mental part, only time would help her health.

He dropped down on the bed of his truck and lay back, staring up into the blue sky. Deep breaths helped calm his heart and his eyes drifted shut. Yet, instead of seeing Mary's Gospel, the image appearing behind his eyelids was Austin Spellsin. Branimir didn't try to chase the picture out of his head. It had been five years since Til's death, and while Branimir hadn't been a monk during that time, he'd never had a man catch his attention as fast as Austin had.

Branimir grunted when his cock filled and pressed against the zipper of his jeans. It wasn't a good time for a hard-on, especially when he couldn't do anything about it. He had three classes to ride in later today. Thank God he wasn't eventing or he'd have no time whatsoever. Giving himself a mental shake, Branimir climbed off the truck bed and strolled to the front of his trailer. There was a small changing room built in and he liked it more than changing in the barns.

Til had always teased him about being a prude or being shy. Shyness or being embarrassed by nakedness wasn't the reason why Branimir chose to change in private. Part of it was his better-than-average-size cock. He'd grown tired of hearing the comments when he changed in locker rooms in school. The other issue was he didn't like having to explain about the ugly scar along the left side of his chest and back.

A scar he received when his father ran him off their ranch. The dominant stallion in any herd doesn't want younger males hanging around. It endangered their opportunity to continue to sire offspring. Not that Branimir planned to sleep with his mother or any of the other women in his herd. Being gay ensured it would never happen, but his father followed generations of genetic instinct and chased him from their land.

He never told Til the entire truth of why he left the family ranch, just that his father hadn't liked the idea of him being gay. Til accepted Branimir's explanation and the lie he told about how he got the scar. Thank God Til was an East coast guy and didn't know what being bitten by a horse looked like compared to being gored by a bull.

Branimir changed, not looking at himself in the mirror attached to the back of the door until he was dressed. Gray streaked his dark brown hair and he sighed. Being a shifter should have kept him immune to age or even the signs of age, but there seemed to be more gray or white in his hair every morning. Crow's feet at the corners of his eyes spoke of days out in the sun.

Picking up his riding helmet, he shook his head and climbed from the trailer. Why was he thinking about all of this now? It had been years since his lover's death and even longer than that since Branimir had thought about his parents. Was the young Spellsin the cause of his thoughts or was it the fact Branimir was getting older and acknowledging his loneliness?

"Hey, Javlosk, great to see you here. I wanted to talk to you about that chestnut gelding you're showing in the immediate hunter class."

Branimir pushed his personal thoughts to the back of his head and let the business part take over. He was at the show to sell horses and to get people interested in his training ability. Being a horse shifter had its advantages when your job was to train them. Til often joked about Branimir being a horse whisperer, and Branimir never let on how close to the truth that was.

"I'm just going to saddle him up, Ranson. You're welcome to join me. Get a closer look at him." Branimir nodded toward his barn.

"Thanks." Ranson walked along side him. "You hear about Billings?"

"Yeah. It's about time the bastard got his ass sent to jail for abuse." Branimir snarled. "I've been trying to get the authorities to do something about him for years."

"There are quite a few of us who are going to talk to the police about him." Ranson shook his head. "Should've known it'd take someone important like Spellsin to get the ball rolling, though. The rest of us aren't shit compared to him."

Branimir nodded. Austin Spellsin's name was synonymous with wealth and power. While the younger Spellsin had made a name for himself in the riding world, the rest of the family built oilrigs and manufactured drilling equipment. Earlier that day was the first time Branimir had talked to Austin, but he'd heard and seen how talented the man was. It didn't matter to Branimir if Austin's money bought him the best horses. A person could buy the most expensive, highly bred mounts in the world, but if he didn't have the talent to ride them, they'd look like nothing more than plow horses.

"True, but does it really matter who got the police's attention, as long as the end result is the same?"

Ranson grunted. "I guess you're right. I know you've been trying to buy Mary's Gospel from Billings for years now. Are you going to see if Spellsin will sell her? That is if the court awards custody to him or the ASPCA."

"The court'll take custody of her, and I'm pretty sure he'll adopt her when they release her. He seemed determined to make sure she has a better life from here on out." Branimir shrugged. "To be honest, it doesn't matter to me who owns her, as long as it isn't Billings. Spellsin's rep says he takes good care of his mounts, and even if he can't ride her, she'll make a great brood mare. She has an excellent pedigree."

They arrived at Branimir's barn and he set his helmet down before grabbing a lead rope and halter.

"I'll get Bucky out. You can look him over while I saddle him."

"Okay."

Branimir settled into the familiar routine of readying a horse for a show. He tried not to think of Mary's Gospel or how drop dead gorgeous her soon-to-be new owner was.

After he groomed and saddled Bucky, he led him out and allowed Ranson to give him a leg up. He put his helmet on and nodded at Ranson.

"I've already made up my mind, but I'd like to see how he handles in the arena."

"Great. You know the price." He chuckled and winked before nudging Bucky to start moving toward the gate.

"Good luck."

Branimir glanced around to see who had shouted to him. Austin sat on a large black-bay mare. He turned Bucky in Austin's direction, approaching him.

"Are you in this class as well? I didn't know you rode in hunter classes."

Austin grinned at him as he pulled up beside him. "I don't. I'm in the jumping class right after yours. I was warming up Sunny here. Thought I'd give you some good luck, though I don't think you'll need it."

"Thanks. Bucky hasn't been doing this for long, but it's something he likes." Branimir rubbed his hand along the gelding's neck.

"He's a thoroughbred, right?" Austin studied what he could see of the horse. "He can't be much older than seven."

"Bucky raced on the track since he was two. They retired him when he was five because of disinterest in his career. Of course, he's a gelding, so there's no reason why he'd get a luxurious retirement. I rescued him from an auction. I outbid a slaughterhouse owner for him and several other horses."

"Really?" The younger man tilted his head as sudden realization flared in his eyes. "That's where I've heard your name and the name of your farm. You rescue retired Thoroughbreds and retrain them for other uses."

"Class four-five-six, please enter the arena." The announcement came over the loudspeaker.

"Well, good luck." Austin smiled and waved.

11

Branimir nodded as he clicked to Bucky to get him moving. He could feel Austin's eyes boring in between his shoulder blades. While he liked the idea of Austin ogling him, he knew he had to keep his focus. Bucky lifted his head and entered the arena like a professional. Branimir knew the gelding wasn't going to set the show world on fire, but he would be great for an amateur rider who wanted to do some weekend shows. Ranson had a daughter who loved horses and would take good care of Bucky. Branimir had sold a couple horses to Ranson before, so he knew Bucky would be taken care of.

He and the other riders trotted around the arena, putting their mounts through their paces. Branimir wiped all thoughts out of his mind except for the class. If anyone knew he was a horse shifter, they might think he'd use his abilities to ensure he'd win every class he entered. Yet he didn't. Cheating wasn't his way. He had enough trust in his horse's talent and his own ability to train them. Also, it didn't matter whether he won anything or not. All that mattered was making sure the horse looked its best.

Unfortunately, he couldn't keep all the horses he retrained or rehabbed. He didn't have enough land, even though Til had bought two farms adjacent to his family farm, adding three hundred acres. Branimir had ten mares and two stallions he kept for his breeding, but he had another fifty horses he rehabbed and twenty he trained for other owners. His reputation allowed him to make enough money to keep everything going and pay the people who worked for him.

So, while he didn't entirely enjoy horse shows, he brought his horses to showcase them and it kept the money flowing. Bucky stumbled slightly, and Branimir gathered him with the reins. He kept his attention on his mount for the rest of the time.

After they finished, Bucky received the third place ribbon and a new owner. Ranson wrote him a check, and Bucky moved to a stall Ranson had rented. Branimir told the gelding good-bye and that he would have a good life with his new rider. The gelding butted his head against Branimir's chest in understanding and happily trotted off with Ranson's groom.

Branimir tucked the check in his pocket before heading back to his barn, helmet under his arm. He hummed softly to himself as he put his helmet down and grabbed a rake. The hunter class had been his last one for the show and he wanted to clean the stall before he left. He'd only brought Bucky this time.

He missed his other horses and his farm. Territory meant a lot to a horse. A place where he felt comfortable and the rest of his herd lived. It was time to go home.

"Heading out so soon?"

He turned to spot Austin standing in the doorway, along with Edward Monterrose and Juan Romanos. After leaning the pitchfork against the stall, he walked over to them.

"Yeah. Bucky's class was my last one, and Ranson bought him, so there's no reason to stick around. Besides, I'm starting to miss my other horses and my home."

"Don't blame you. We wondered if you'd like to go get a drink with us. We're sort of celebrating finally getting Billings arrested." Austin gestured at Juan and Edward.

Smiling, Branimir shook his head. "I'd love to, guys, but I have to get home. I'm going to drive straight through. I've got two rescues coming in tomorrow and I want to be around when they get there."

Juan slapped his shoulder with a grin. "Totally understandable. A friend of my uncle's takes in rescues as well. Maybe you've heard of Leslie Hardin."

"Who hasn't? He was one of the best riders/trainers on the East Coast before his accident. Is he the one who sponsored you?" Branimir grabbed one of his tack trunks.

"Well, he used a few of his contacts to get me started when he figured out how interested in jumping I was. Got me in contact with Eddie." Juan nudged Eddie with an elbow.

"It's a spider web of connections," Eddie commented. "Somehow our families are all involved with each other."

Branimir laughed. "Sounds like fun in a way. Having people who care about you."

Austin nodded.

"I have to go, but if you need help, Austin, you know how to get a hold of me."

He shook hands with the three men and headed out. If he drove straight through, he'd been home by early morning.

CHAPTER 2

A truck and trailer drove up the driveway and stopped next to the main barn. Branimir walked out to greet the man climbing slowly out of the truck. Austin limped toward him with his hand out.

"Thanks for agreeing to help me with Mary."

They shook hands, and Branimir looked down at the soft cast covering Austin's ankle. "No problem, man, but what happened to you?"

Austin chuckled. "Fell off one of my horses. Twisted my ankle and banged up my hip bad enough I can't ride for a while."

Branimir winced. "That's tough. The horse take a wrong step or something?"

"Nah. It was my fault. I wasn't paying attention to what I was doing, and he was an inexperienced horse, so he came at a fence at the wrong angle because I didn't correct him. He was smart enough to know he wasn't going to make it, and he refused. I fell off, which hasn't happened to me in a long time."

Austin shook his head and grinned, while Branimir smiled.

"I've had that happen a time or two. Come on...let's get her settled and put your foot up." Branimir went to the back of the trailer and opened the doors.

Mary's Gospel shifted as Branimir laid his hand on her hip. Anxiety shot through him and he realized the mare was worried about what he might do to her. She remembered being stuck in a confined place for days without anywhere to move or food to eat. She didn't know who did it to her or why, and to a horse the why didn't factor into her thoughts. All she knew was she'd been hurt and trapped in a small space before.

She snorted as Branimir slid up to the front of the trailer. He reached out to touch her nose and she tossed it away from him.

"It's okay, honey," he murmured. "I won't hurt you."

The horse eyed Branimir suspiciously. She'd been hit about the head too many times to trust this new person, though something about this human was different. He smelled more like a horse than most of the others she'd run into. His mumbling intrigued her and she eased closer to hear those words, even though she didn't understand them.

Branimir slid his hand up and clipped a lead rope to her halter before clicking softly. With a snort, she backed out in a wild surge, wincing each time her hips or sides brushed the trailer walls. Mary hated it. Didn't matter that the trailer she was leaving was far bigger than the one she'd been captured in. The mare dashed out the last few feet to dance around at the end of the rope.

There wasn't any pressure to keep her still or stop her. Finally, her energy ran out and she stood, legs trembling and chest heaving. Mary's head dropped and she closed her eyes as the man stepped closer and rubbed her shoulder. She shuddered at the touch, but didn't fight it.

"Come on, my lady. We'll get you settled in."

Branimir gestured for Austin to follow him as he led the mare into the barn and her new stall. After taking the halter off, he made sure she had hay and water. Austin leaned against the wall, watching as Branimir strolled down the aisle, petting each horse's nose and speaking softly.

When he finished, he took Austin's elbow and let the younger man lean on him as they made their way up to the main house. Austin wrapped his arm around Branimir's shoulder.

"I appreciate you helping me. Not only with Mary, but with this as well." Austin waved a hand at his ankle.

"I've needed help before, so it's no big deal to pay it back to someone else." Branimir helped Austin sit down at the table in the kitchen. "Would you like some coffee?"

"Sure."

Branimir puttered around the kitchen, getting the coffee made and pulling out some sandwich stuff from the refrigerator. "I had breakfast at, like, five this morning. Would you like something to eat as well?"

"Yes, please. I have some muscle relaxants I need to take." Austin rubbed the back of his neck. "I was wondering if I could stick around for a couple days while you work with Mary. I can't ride until my hip's better."

Setting the plates on the table, he thought about Austin's request. He rarely had anyone, except the people who worked for him, stay around, unless they were there to buy a horse. His methods for rehabbing the worst cases weren't observable by men. While he didn't think Mary's Gospel would need those drastic methods, he didn't want to risk it.

He met Austin's questioning gaze and the clear blue of his eyes touched Branimir in a way he hadn't been effected since Til died. He hadn't shut himself off from company, but he'd never been interested in something lasting.

"All right. You're more than welcome to stay. I have guest rooms you can use." Branimir created his own sandwich and took a bite.

"Thanks. I'm also looking for a horse."

"Don't you have enough horses to ride? Plus you can go to a top-level breeder and get a mount with blue blood instead a damaged horse from me." He shrugged and sipped his coffee.

"Not for me. I have more than enough mounts at the moment, not including Mary. I'm looking to get one for my niece. She's a good young rider, and I want to give her a horse she can grow with. One who will learn as she does. The one she's riding now knows as much, if not more than she does and that's fine. But I'd like to get her another one." Austin ate some of his sandwich.

Branimir looked up and smiled. "It must be nice to have an uncle who cares so much about you, he's willing to spend a lot of money on you."

He winked as Austin reached over and punched him in the arm.

"We Spellsins know how to take care of our family." The younger man sat back, grimacing as he hit his ankle on the chair. "How about you? Do you have any family to take care of?"

Branimir pursed his lips and shook his head. "It's just me. My partner died about five years ago in a car accident. So the horses are my family."

"Sorry to hear that, man. I never met Tilman, just saw him around the shows and heard good things about what you were doing here." Austin waved a hand in the general direction of the barns. "I have to ask. Was the rehab center his idea or yours? From what I remember, Tilman's family bred horses. They didn't take in rescued horses and rehabilitate them."

Branimir stood, grabbing their plates and carrying them to the sink. "No, it was my idea. I'd left the family ranch about two years before I met Til. On the new ranch I worked on, we bred horses, but I never really got into that part of it. I liked training them, seeing if I could take an animal everyone's discarded and retrain it. That's how Til and I met. He came out to Montana to check out one of my rescues."

The sound of Austin shifting in his chair caused Branimir to turn around. The jealousy and sadness in the man's expression surprised Branimir. What could Austin be envious or sad about? It wasn't like they knew each other.

"Was it love at first sight?"

Pausing, Bran thought about his relationship with Tilman Harlan. His lover had been the quintessential Southern gentleman, yet he didn't hesitate to seduce Branimir when he saw how interested Branimir had been in him. Of course, back then men weren't as open as they were now, especially in ranch country, so they hid their encounters until Til had to return home. At the time, Branimir had agonized over the choice of staying or going with Til. How scary the decision had seemed then, but even though Til had been gone for so long now, Branimir didn't regret one minute of their life together. They'd had fifteen great years. Oh, they'd fought because no relationship was perfect, but Branimir liked who he was when he had Til.

"I'm sorry. I didn't mean to bring up sad memories."

He glanced over at Austin and grinned. "You didn't. There aren't any sad memories for me about Til. Sure, I still miss him, but I've come to terms with his death. I did my grieving. To answer your question, I'm not sure it was love at first sight, but it was definitely lust. Til was different from the cowboys I'd worked around all my life. Dressed and talked different. He was confident of who he was, inside and out."

"I envy you," Austin admitted, fidgeting with the frayed ends of a hole in his jeans. "I've never really had anyone, friend or otherwise, who made me feel like you obviously felt for Tilman."

Branimir strolled back to Austin and rested his hand on the man's shoulder. "I was twenty when I met Til. Some people are lucky to find love when they're young. Others, it takes a while, but I have no doubt you'll find someone."

Their gazes met, and something shifted inside Branimir. An emotion he'd felt before welled up in him, but he controlled it. Smiling, he stepped back from Austin. If he was falling in love again, he wanted to take it slowly. No matter what Austin said, he might not be ready to settle for one man and one place.

"Why don't we go get your bag and settle you in? I have some work to do, but I'll give you a tour of the barns before I get started."

"Sounds good."

Austin pushed himself to his feet and limped after Branimir. They dropped his stuff off in his room and headed out to the main barn.

"Mary looks good. She's put on weight."

"It's not the weight that's the problem. Any horse will eat as long as they have food in front of them and they aren't sick. She's a good eater. Had to keep an eye on her for a little while at first, but as the month went by, she put on some flesh and the vet figured she was out of the woods health-wise." Austin shook his head as they entered the barn. "Mentally, she doesn't want to have anything to do with humans. She'd be happy standing in her stall or hanging out in a paddock all day. I'm not even sure she likes other horses."

Branimir nodded at one of his grooms as they went by. "It's possible she hasn't been exposed to them in a good context. I'll watch her for a couple days to figure out the best way to approach her without adding more stress. Once I have a game plan, I'll start introducing her to things to re-condition her to good experiences. I have some retirees on the farm who might be good for her to hang out with."

"Retirees?" Austin stopped when he spotted a big black horse hanging its head over a stall door. "Oh my, where did this guy come from?"

Shaking his head, Branimir lead the way over to the gelding. "You don't want to know. It wasn't pretty, but I got to him in time and now we're hoping to find a good home for him. He's another like Mary. Won't win for looks, but he can jump and flat-out run if you need him to."

He stood back and watched Austin interact with the horse. He'd never heard any rumors about Austin abusing his mounts, but sometimes it paid to see the man in action. Branimir planned to spy on Austin as well. People behaved when they knew others watched them. He wanted to see how Austin acted when he didn't think anyone was looking.

Not that he didn't think Austin was a good guy. Branimir's instincts rarely led him astray and they told him Austin was kind and gentle, but firm when he needed to be.

"Hey, Bran," one of the stable hands called out to him, "I see we got a new horse. Do you want her to stay in this barn or should she be moved out to the white barn?"

"For the moment, we'll keep her up here. She needs to get used to people again without the angry words and hitting. After a week or two, we'll see if she needs special treatment. Oh, can you open the paddock door in her stall? She needs to be able to run around. Put Sparky in the paddock beside her," Branimir ordered.

"Yes, sir." Jose nodded as he went to do what Branimir said.

"Sparky?" Austin shot him a look.

"Yeah. He's one of the retirees I told you about. Bought him at a horse auction. He was heading to slaughter, and I couldn't let him go. I could tell he had several good years ahead of him. Sparky might not be able to be ridden, but he's pretty laid back, so I use him for some of the more excitable horses."

"I wouldn't call Mary excitable," Austin commented.

"No, but she's afraid and nervous. Sparky will begin to teach her not all humans will try to hurt you. Like us humans, she just needs someone to show her there are other realities out there and we can all get a happy ending if we're willing to meet others half way."

*   *   *

"Good thought."

Austin watched Branimir as the older man murmured to his horses. Even after being suitably impressed with Branimir when they'd met a month ago, he'd done his research before bringing Mary to him. The mare had been through enough trauma already; she didn't need anymore.

When Austin gained custody of the mare, he explained to his father it didn't matter if he could compete with Mary's Gospel or not. All that mattered was she be healed outside and in. Also, he wanted her to be happy. He understood it was a strange concept for most people to grasp, but what was the point of owning animals if he didn't want them to be as happy as they made him? He'd tried explaining that to his dad, but it didn't work. His dad didn't see animals as having feelings and he didn't see Austin's horses as pets. They made the family money, and in the end, that was all his dad care about.

"Have you thought about what discipline you'd like to train Mary for?" Branimir grabbed the halter and lead rope from the hook at the front of the black gelding's stall. He slipped in with the horse and slid the halter on the horse before attaching the lead rope to bring him out. Austin stepped back and to the side.

"I think she'd be a good eventer. I'm not sure what plans Billings had for her, besides ruining her."

Austin studied the gelding after Branimir clipped the black into the crossties and retrieved a box of grooming items from the tack room. The gelding stood seventeen hands, which was taller than any of Austin's other mounts. Deep chest and well-muscled haunches spoke of power and stamina. His black coat was marred with scars, yet he held his head high. It was the same look Austin saw in Mary's eyes when he looked at the mare. It said they'd been beaten and bruised, but they weren't broken. Their spirit still burned brightly inside.

While Mary had a way to go to relearn how to trust humans, it was apparent the gelding understood. He let Austin pet him without shying away or cowering in fear. Branimir handed Austin a currycomb.

"You help me groom Buster here, and we'll saddle him up. I'll take him out in the arena and you can get a look at his gaits."

"He's a little bigger than I was thinking for my niece." Austin took the comb and started working on Buster's left side.

"Oh, I don't think he'd work for your niece. He's calm now, but he can get nervous out on course or in the ring. He needs a firmer hand than your niece is ready to give right now."

The grin Branimir shot him over Buster's back landed like a punch to his gut. Austin inhaled sharply, trying to ignore his erection. While he did think Branimir was no doubt the sexiest man he'd see in a long time, he wasn't sure the man was looking for anything, and Austin didn't do one-night stands or flings.

He wasn't opposed to them, just didn't do them. Seen too many turn nasty or awkward. Plus he didn't have time, not even for a quickie. He had too many classes to ride in at too many shows. Austin wouldn't complain, though. He'd much rather have *his* life than working in the family business. He wasn't meant for the corporate world. Thank God, his father understood that and let Austin do what he wanted.

"You might know someone who would be interested in this guy. He'd make a marvelous intermediate dressage horse. His last owner crashed the trailer Buster rode in and injured him, so he's not fluid enough to make it at Grand Prix level." Branimir gestured to a jagged scar running almost the length of Buster's leg.

Austin looked closer. "I'm surprised they didn't put him down right there. That's one nasty looking scar."

"They might have, but the first cop on the scene happened to love horses and he called a vet in right away. When the vet got there, they somehow managed to stabilize him before they transported him to a clinic. They called me, and I agreed to foot the bill to get him healed up enough. The police arrested his owner for drunk driving, and I got a pretty good horse out of the deal."

"Shit. That had to cost you a lot out of pocket for him." Austin finished brushing and took the pad Branimir handed him.

Branimir shrugged. "I don't brag about it, but I'm not hurting for cash. The breeding operation pays for itself, and I do pretty well with retraining and selling the horses to new owners. Plus I have money coming in from other sources. I don't believe in putting all my eggs into one basket, even if I prefer the horses to any of the other things."

Austin laughed. "So do I. My father swears I'm a throwback to my cowboy ancestors."

They finished saddling Buster before sliding the bit into the gelding's mouth. Austin took the reins to lead the horse over to the outdoor arena. Branimir grabbed a helmet and gloves on the way. Austin watched the older man hook the chinstrap.

"Wouldn't take you as a guy who wore a helmet outside the show ring," he commented.

Branimir took a leg up from him and settled into the dressage saddle like he was coming home. The man looked like he belonged on Buster's back, and Austin had a feeling Branimir would look like that on any horse.

"I saw too many serious injuries caused when people didn't wear the right head gear. Might take away from my cowboy image, but I'd rather be safe than sorry."

"I'm with you on that, man." Austin slapped Branimir's thigh, doing his best to ignore the hard muscle under the jeans. "Show me what the big boy can do."

The wicked wink Branimir sent him made Austin think about what he'd said. *Holy shit!* Could he have sounded more suggestive? Yet he was surprised Branimir caught it. The man seemed wrapped up in his horses and not looking for a hook-up.

Austin swallowed hard, his eyes glued to the firm ass rising and falling above the saddle as Buster trotted around the perimeter of the arena. He shifted in such a way Branimir couldn't see him adjust the hard-on in his riding breeches. Why did he have to wear such tight pants today?

Forcing his mind off the movement of Branimir, Austin focused on Buster's stride and fluidity as Branimir steered the gelding through some of the movements of a third-level test. Buster's collection was exceptional, being on the bit and accepting it without fighting Branimir's instruction.

At the extended trot, Buster floated over the ground and when he turned in through the diagonal to do his flying lead changes, it looked like he skipped across the arena. His ears flickered back toward Branimir and forward as he showed off.

Austin could see a little stiffness in his side during the leg yields and half-passes, but most of it could be worked out the more training the gelding had. His elasticity seemed compromised by the scars on his chest, but still Austin agreed with Branimir. Buster didn't have the flash and presence a Grand Prix dressage horse needed to succeed at the highest levels. Yet he had more than enough talent to make an amateur rider a great mount.

He dug out his phone and dialed a number, while keeping an eye on the pair in the arena. Branimir loosened the reins, allowing Buster to free walk around. The gelding stretched and yawned like this was all so boring to him. Branimir's laughter rang through the air, freezing Austin with the phone pressed to his ear.

The sheer joy on the man's face tugged at Austin's heart and gave him the feeling the only time Branimir really laughed and enjoyed life was while working with his horses. It wasn't like Branimir was sad or anything like that. Austin got the idea Branimir had worked through his anger and sadness at Til's death. The other man seemed lonely…or maybe the right word was solitary.

"Spellsin? Are you there? You better not have butt dialed me again."

His cousin's voice broke through his thoughts.

"Shit! Sorry about that, Nelson. Got thinking about something else there for a minute."

"Why am I not surprised?" His cousin chuckled. "So what's got you calling me?"

"A man with a horse."

Austin smiled at Branimir as he and Buster walked by. His cousin grunted.

"Who's the man? What kind of horse?"

"The man is Branimir Javlosk and the horse is Buster. Well, I suppose he has a regular name, but his barn name is Buster. He's seventeen hands, black, and a solid third-level dressage horse. With a little work, I think he could be a great Intermediate horse."

Nelson stayed quiet for a few minutes, and Austin figured his cousin was trying to fit the name with a face.

"Does Javlosk run that rescue and rehab place up in Paris?"

"That's the one. I think Buster would fit Mrs. Williamson pretty well." Austin leaned his arms on the top rail of the fence and braced his injured foot on the bottom rail to take some weight off it. "You should see if she might be interested in driving down to check him out."

"He that good?"

"I'll see if Branimir will let me videotape him putting Buster through his paces and I'll send it to you, so you can decide if he'll even be worth the time. The only thing I'll tell you up front is he won't win any conformation classes."

"Roman nosed? Hammer-headed? Parrot-mouthed?"

"Quit listing shit. He was in a serious trailer accident when he was younger. Scarred him up pretty good, which is why he won't be more than Intermediate. His elasticity and fluidity are compromised because of the injuries." Austin waved Branimir over to him. "I can have Branimir give you some vitals on him."

"Sure. You've always had a good eye for matching horses and riders. I'd like to see the video and then we'll see about getting Mrs. Williamson down to look at him."

Austin held out the phone to Branimir. "It's my cousin. He has a client who might be interested in buying Buster. Nelson just needs some information from you."

Branimir dismounted and held the reins out to Austin. "Can you take him back to the barn? Take his tack off and brush him out for me?"

"Certainly."

Austin limped away, leading Buster, while Branimir talked with Nelson. By the time he'd finished brushing the gelding, Branimir returned with a smile on his face. He handed Austin his phone before slapping him on the shoulder.

"Thanks a lot. I knew you'd have an idea who might want Buster." Branimir unhooked Buster and returned him to his stall, hanging the halter on the hook outside the door.

"Are we going to videotape him tomorrow maybe?" Austin slowly followed Branimir down the aisle to an office, where he dropped onto the ragged tan couch with a sigh.

Branimir sat in the chair behind the desk and shook his head. "I don't need to. I already have a video of him at a show a couple months ago. He took second, so it was a good day for him."

Austin let his head fall back and he closed his eyes as his hip and ankle began to throb. He jerked upright when strong hands grabbed his legs. He opened his eyes to see Branimir lifting his legs to rest them on the couch.

"You've been doing too much walking around. Why don't you put your legs up and rest? I'm going to be in and out, working some of the horses. Do you need any pills or anything?"

"I left my medicine in my room. I'm due for a pain killer about now."

Branimir nodded. "Okay. I'll go and get it for you. Unless you want to go lie down in your room."

Austin thought for a moment. "Yeah. That's probably for the best. I don't want to get in your way out here."

He gasped as Branimir scooped him up into his arms and started to carry him to the house.

"Holy shit! Wait a minute. I can walk and I've got to be heavy, man. You're going to hurt yourself carting my ass around like this."

Branimir pressed his lips to Austin's ear and whispered, "What if I like carrying you like this? What if I wish I was taking you to bed for a different reason?"

Holy fuck!

CHAPTER 3

The shudder rocking Austin's body drew Branimir's attention and he remembered why he was carrying the man. He shook his head at himself. Yes, he wanted Austin with a lust bordering on addiction. The emotions racing through him reminded him of how he felt when he first saw Til. Who knew if Austin would come to mean as much to Branimir as Til did, but still he was happy to be attracted to someone. Horses weren't meant to be alone, and neither were horse shifters. They needed their herd to make them completely happy.

"Sorry. Now isn't the time to start anything with you. You're injured, and we should get to know each other a little better before I drag you off to my bed."

Austin blinked those pretty blue eyes, and Branimir bit his lip to keep from moaning. He tightened his grip on Austin's hard body, but immediately loosened it when the other man winced.

"Forgot about the bruises there for a moment. Here's your room."

He shouldered open the door and set Austin down on the edge of the bed. He stepped back and tucked his hands in his pockets before he started stripping Austin.

"Do you need any help?"

Austin tipped his head and studied Branimir for a moment, causing Branimir to fight the urge to scuff his boots on the carpet. What was Austin thinking? The teasing gleam in the man's eyes told Branimir asking him for help had crossed his mind, and it wouldn't be just a simple getting ready to take a nap. It would be a full out seduction.

Branimir lifted one eyebrow, and Austin smirked.

"Okay. I'll be good for now." Austin pouted for a second before grinning. "I can take it from here. I'll take my meds and make some phone calls to check in on my horses. Come and get me for dinner?"

"Will do." He couldn't resist reaching out and brushing the back of his fingers along the edge of Austin's jaw. "Call me if you need anything. I have my cell with me all the time."

"I'll do that. Go on. I didn't mean to take up time you could be spending with the horses."

Branimir left before he crawled into bed with Austin and snuggled with the slender man.

Dashing down the stairs, he jogged out into the fresh air and breathed deeply. Tonight, he'd run off the excess energy his desire for Austin built within him. Thank God for several acres of privately owned forested land. He often ran the trails at night. So far no one reported seeing a horse running free. If that ever happened, he'd have to come up with a good story, but he'd been lucky since he moved to the farm.

"Hey, boss, we're ready to get started."

Looking up, Branimir spied four of his employees standing in the outdoor arena with their first mounts for the day. He had written out the training schedule earlier that morning and posted it on the bulletin board just inside the barn.

"Great. Let me get my notebook and we'll get started."

He kept notes on all the horses in his barn, whether they were rehabbing or training them. It helped when it came to selling them because he could tell potential buyers all the animal's quirks and habits. Also, it helped matched owners and mounts. He didn't ever want to find out he sold one of his horses to someone who abused or didn't love them.

After snatching up his notebook, he strolled out of the barn and climbed up on the platform he'd built on one side of the arena. It gave him a perfect view of the entire area without getting in the way. Tomorrow, he'd set up the digital camera and tape their different tests. Another thing that helped when he had people looking for mounts.

"All right, everyone, mount up and warm up. After warm-up, I want Lissa and Spots to go first. Take the mare through a test. I don't care which one. You know what Spots is capable of. I think she was hesitating entering into the extension at a trot. Steady her and let her know you're supporting her. She should be able to move into it without pausing," he called out to Lissa.

"Yes, sir." The dark-haired girl encouraged the Appaloosa mare to stretch her muscles and make her connection with her rider.

Branimir watched as the trio of riders and mounts trotted and walked around the arena until he blew his whistle and two of them moved out of the rectangular area. Lissa urged Spots to trot down the centerline to where they stopped perfectly. The girl saluted and continued on to the end of the arena.

Spots did everything Lissa asked of her with her neck arched and beautiful propulsion through her canter, yet, like Branimir had said, she hesitated as she started her extended trot.

"Stop, Lissa. She needs to be more collected as you push her into the extension. I think that's where the problem is."

For the rest of the day, Branimir worked with riders and horses, finding the best way to get both to respond and bond with each other. The best rider/horse combinations were the ones where the trust between them was palpable. Where, as a spectator, he knew the horse would do anything or jump anything the rider put in front of him because the horse trusted the rider with his life.

Branimir finished his last training session and returned the notebooks to his office. He'd transcribe what he wrote in the morning. He picked up a new grooming box before heading toward Mary's stall.

He'd seen her out in the paddock a couple of times during the day. She hadn't been interested in Sparky at first. Actually, she'd tended toward aggression when she spotted him, but he pretended indifference and she'd slowly ended up accepting the gelding being beside her paddock.

When he leaned over the door, she was standing in the opened doorway with her head outside. He saw her tremble and he wondered what had scared her. He coughed, not wanting to frighten her by slipping into the stall without her knowing. She swung her head around and studied him with her bright, fear-filled eyes.

"It's all right, honey. Your days of abuse are over."

Branimir could almost see the skepticism in her eyes. He chuckled as he shook his head. Mary might listen to him, or feel the confidence he felt when he said those words, but it would take a while before she believed him.

Mary's fear would last until she relearned how to trust humans. It wouldn't happen overnight, not even with Branimir's closer connection with her. Admittedly, her nature made her more inclined to trust him and reach out for his approval because he'd established he was the herd stallion. Yet she'd had her reservations beaten into her over several years and the walls she'd built wouldn't be easy for him to climb.

Taking his time, he slipped the halter over her head and fastened it, stopping and waiting each time she tensed or snorted. There wasn't any forcing her to accept it if she didn't want it on. Billings must have beaten her around the head often, given how much Mary didn't want Branimir anywhere near her head.

He stepped away, holding out a carrot in the palm of his hand to reward her. The mare trembled, but lipped it up before jerking her head away. Branimir kept up his soft chatter. She needed to get used to a gentle voice and touch after being yelled at and hit every time a human approached her.

After an hour, he led her from her stall and clipped her into the crossties. She wasn't as nervous, but still she tensed each time he came near her. Branimir opened the grooming box and dug through it, making sure Mary could see what he did. He didn't want to surprise her. He picked up a currycomb and stood in front of the mare, holding it out so she could smell it.

She lipped it once before turning her attention to the horses in their stalls. Taking it as a sign, he moved to her right shoulder and started brushing her. He quickly got lost in the soothing job of grooming. Her hipbones stuck out, along with her ribs, but he could see where she'd put weight on. Mary still needed several hundred more pounds to be at a healthy weight, but she looked better than she did when he saw her a month ago.

"Austin's been treating you good, honey. You certainly lucked out when you got him as a new owner. I think you'll be a good fit together. Sweetheart, you have the soul of a fighter and you'll soar over those jumps like a bird once we get you in a better place mentally."

Branimir set the brush back in the box. No dropping it or sudden movements. Mary wouldn't stand for that, and it upset the other horses as well. He grabbed the hoof pick and bent to touch her fetlock on her right foreleg. She lifted it without a fight, and he nodded. At least he wouldn't have to argue with her about that. Some horses, even those who hadn't been abused, hated to have their hooves cleaned.

He picked out each hoof and combed out her mane and tail before taking her back into her stall. He removed the halter, gave her some more carrots and left, watching from outside the box to see what she would do. Mary sniffed the fresh hay and water before burying her nose in the bucket of oats he'd brought her, while the others fed the rest of the horses in the barn.

The barn was filled with the sounds of munching as the horses ate their dinner. He hung Mary's halter on the hook outside her stall and returned her grooming box to the tack room. He checked in with the night grooms who hung around to keep an eye on the pregnant mares, in case they foaled during the night and needed help.

Everything looked good, so he headed back to the big house and entered the mudroom in the back by the kitchen. He stripped his boots off, along with his dirty T-shirt and jeans. Branimir tossed them into the laundry basket he kept in the room for that very reason. He tugged on a clean shirt and a pair of sweats before padding barefoot into the kitchen.

Austin stood, propped next to the stove, stirring a pot of stew. Branimir leaned over and sniffed, breathing in the delicious scent. He grinned at Austin.

"I might've gotten the better end of this deal if you cook like this all the time."

He swore the younger man blushed, but Austin winked, so he wasn't sure.

"Need to keep my horse's trainer happy." Austin nodded toward the table. "I set the table, but if you want some salad, you'll have to make it yourself. Haven't gotten around to it yet."

"You do know you don't have to cook for me? I am capable of making edible food." Branimir opened the refrigerator and pulled out all the salad makings.

Austin chuckled. "I figured you could cook. You definitely don't look like you're starving or anything, but since I can't ride, I need to do something to keep from getting bored."

Branimir started chopping. "I'm not complaining, honey. If you get tired of it, just let me know. I'm more than willing to cook."

He ducked his head when Austin turned to look at him. *Honey?* Why did the endearment slip out? He'd tried to keep his growing attraction low-key, but it seemed he couldn't quite control his mouth.

Austin must've chosen not to say anything because he changed the subject. "Did you work with Mary today?"

"Yes. I groomed her and put her back in her stall. She has issues with people touching her head, so putting her halter on took some time, but she doesn't mind being groomed or having her hooves cleaned." Branimir dumped the salad stuff into a bowl and carried it over to the

29

table. "Is the stew ready?"

"Can you dish it out? My ankle's aching."

Turning to look at Austin, Branimir saw the lines of pain around the man's mouth and forehead. He rushed over to wrap his arm around Austin's waist, letting the man lean on him as they headed back to the table.

"Next time say something. I don't mind doing the running around while you rest up."

Austin put his ankle up on one of the chairs and sighed. "I know. I'm just used to doing stuff on my own. I forget to ask for help when I need it."

Branimir dropped to his knee next to Austin's chair. He took the man's hand in his and squeezed. "I'd rather you ordered me around all the time than risk you hurting yourself even more."

With that pronouncement, he leaned forward and pressed their lips together.

*   *   *

Shock rippled through Austin. Not that he didn't want Branimir to kiss him, but he hadn't been expecting it. His mind blanked as Branimir slid his hand around to cup the back of his head and took their kiss deeper.

He leaned closer, moaning softly as Branimir's tongue swept in to tease his own and stroke along his teeth. He'd never thought his teeth would be an erogenous zone, but apparently anywhere Branimir touched turned Austin on. His cock stiffened and pressed against his zipper.

Austin shifted to take the pressure off and pain zinged through him as he tweaked his hip. He grunted, and Branimir eased away, concern shining in his brown eyes.

"Are you okay?"

"Yeah," Austin forced out from between gritted teeth. "Just moved wrong, and now I have blue balls because we can't do anything until my hip's better."

Branimir grinned before pushing to his feet with a grimace. Austin reached out to rest his hand on top of Branimir's.

"Are you all right?"

"Same blue balls problem you have." Branimir gestured to the bulge in the front of his jeans. "Also, getting old is hell on the body, especially if you've been riding most of your life like me. It's my knees giving me pain these days."

Austin nodded as he watched Branimir finish dishing out their supper. Like with any athlete, joints tended to be the biggest problem. He wasn't as old as Branimir, but he did have issues with his knees and ankles.

"So how about we just rub Ben-Gay on each other tonight," he joked.

Branimir laughed and joined him at the table. "Not sure. It might get you pretty excited and I'm not sure your hip's up to that much movement. But I tell you what, tonight before you go to sleep, I'll give you a massage. That should help with your back because I know it's tight from compensating for your hip."

"Anything to get your hands on me."

Austin winked, and Branimir shook his head before digging into their food. The silence filling the room was comfortable. Austin didn't feel the need to fill the air with small talk like he usually did. He was a champion small talker, having done so much of it mingling with sponsors and clients at charity events and shows. Also, he'd learned the talent at a young age for his family's business.

Branimir sighed and sat back in his chair. "That was great, Austin. You can cook for me any time you want."

"Glad you like it. As odd as it might sound coming from me, I like to cook."

Standing, Branimir looked at him. "Why would that be odd?"

Shrugging, Austin lowered his foot and started to stand as well. "Coming from the family I do, people can assume I had cooks and housekeepers all my life."

"Why don't you either sit and keep me company while I clean up or go into the living room and get comfortable on the couch?"

"I'll stay here. I like talking to you." He blushed slightly after admitting his feelings. God, one would think he was a virgin, the way he kept blushing around Branimir.

"Good. I like you being around. Anyway, I don't assume anything. Til's family might not have been as rich as yours, but they were pretty well-off, and yet his mother made him learn how to cook and clean for himself. She said it was because she never wanted him to take their place in society for granted. His parents are pretty good people."

The soft smile gracing Branimir's face told Austin how much the man liked his late lover's family.

"Are they still alive? Do you talk to them often?"

Branimir opened the dishwasher before turning the water on to rinse the plates. "I talk to Til's mom every Sunday. We try to get together for the holidays if I'm free. They moved to Arizona a couple years ago. They said they wanted warmer weather. I think they couldn't stand being around here without Til. I don't blame them."

"Do you talk to your own family very often?"

"No. I haven't talked to anyone in my family in over twenty years, since I moved East to be with Til."

Sadness pooled in Austin's heart. He couldn't imagine not talking to his family. He chatted with all of them, even cousins, on a daily basis. Struggling to his feet, he shuffled over to where Branimir stood at the sink. He wrapped his arms around the older man's waist and buried his face in Branimir's shirt between his shoulder blades.

"I'm sorry," Austin whispered.

Branimir relaxed into Austin's embrace, letting him take a little bit of his weight for a second. "Don't be. It wasn't because I was gay or anything. I left because it was time and I loved Til. I don't miss them and I have Til's family, plus the people I work with. The horses are my family as well. I'm not lonely."

No, Branimir wasn't lonely, but even though Austin hadn't spent much time with him, Austin decided Branimir was the most solitary man he knew. While he was sure Branimir didn't mind being solitary, Austin bet the man didn't like being lonely, which was why he spent so much time with his horses.

He straightened and pressed a kiss at the nape of Branimir's neck before stepping back. At that moment, Austin made a vow to himself. He'd never allow Branimir to be isolated again. He would surround the man with friendship and laughter until a smile was a permanent fixture on Branimir's face. If things were to go beyond friendship, Austin wouldn't complain because he could already tell he would enjoy making love with Branimir.

His heart skipped a beat when Branimir smiled at him over his shoulder and turned back to finish the dishes. *Oh, my God!* Austin's heart was in serious danger if a simple smile from Branimir made him weak in the knees.

After making his way out to the living room, Austin dropped onto the couch and leaned forward to brace his elbows on his knees. He covered his face with his hands and took a deep breath.

When he decided to come to Freeland Farms, he didn't plan on falling for the owner. Not that it caused any problems or anything like that. Austin was single and he was out to the world. He had nothing to hide, but something told him Branimir was a very private person.

How did such a person hook up with Tilman Harlan in the first place? Tilman didn't know the meaning of private or discreet. Oh, Tilman hadn't been flamboyant or obnoxious. He'd just been very extroverted and personable. Maybe Tilman had been the face of the farm, while Branimir was the magic behind how well trained all the Freeland Farms horses were.

Austin looked up as Branimir joined him on the couch, holding out a beer. "Thanks."

"No problem. Are you okay? You looked a little weird when you left the kitchen."

Branimir held his head up and to the side, studying Austin in a way that reminded Austin of how Mary's Gospel looked at him from time to time.

"I'm fine. Just a little freaked out by how easy this is." He gestured between them.

The older man smiled and caught his hand in a loose grip. "Sometimes attraction doesn't have to be hard. Sometimes it can be as easy as watching the sun set. Comfortable and a little exciting to see what the night will bring. I'm not into making things difficult for us, Austin. It's not the way I'm built."

"Will you tell me how the hell you met Tilman? You're so totally opposite from him."

"Like I said earlier, he came out to Montana to check out one of my rescues. I'm not sure if you remember Til's horse, Freeland's Skipper?"

Austin pursed his lips and nodded. "Yeah. Mid-sized bay stallion. Jumped like he had springs in his legs."

"That's him. Anyway, Skipper was a rescue. Bought him at auction to keep him from going to slaughter. He was only seven years old. Much too young to be chopped up for food. Trailered him home and found out just how stubborn he was. If Skipper didn't want to do something, he would fight you to a standstill to keep from doing it." Branimir chuckled. "He was the perfect fit for Til. I got his stubbornness pointed in the right direction, and Til took him from there."

Austin shifted slightly, bringing their shoulders into contact. Branimir rested their hands on his own knee as they relaxed.

"I remember how impressed I was the first time I saw them

compete. Do you still have Skipper?"

"Yeah. He's one of our foundation studs for the Freeland line. He's slowing down a little, so I don't have him cover as many mares as he used to. I might retire him soon and let him live like a king in his paddock. He's the oldest one of the breeding stock." Branimir laid his head back on the cushions and smiled as Austin snuggled closer.

Austin breathed in the warm horse-and man-scented aroma drifting from Branimir's skin. He knew a lot of people wouldn't find it attractive or desirable, but for Austin, it was more than that. It soothed him in a way nothing else could. It gave him a sense of home because, at times, horses were the only friends he'd had, especially when he was younger and in school.

Being a Spellsin didn't mean his life was charmed and nothing bad ever happened to him. He was bullied and picked on at the boarding school until he finally told his father what was going on. His father pulled him and sent him to a public school where things weren't as bad, but they weren't perfect either.

Being teased because he was gay would have been one thing, and he might have dealt with it on his own, but the kids at the public school gave him shit because he was a Spellsin. He ended up spending most of his after-school time at the stables on his father's country estate.

Turning his head, he buried his nose in the crook of Branimir's neck and inhaled deeply. Branimir laughed as he reached over to encourage Austin to sit on his lap. He wrapped his arms around Branimir's waist and they cuddled, just listening to each other breathe for a little while.

"Til didn't hide his attraction for me, and I didn't mind. I'd known for a while it was time to head out and find some place else to live and work. I let him know how I felt, and the rest is history as they say. I was perfectly happy moving to Kentucky. I couldn't argue with the quality of horses I got to work with either."

"Do you ever get homesick? Is your family still alive?"

Branimir snorted. "I get homesick for the open skies and mountains of Montana. The scenery and all that, but I don't really miss my family that much. I've built my own here. There've been great times and terrible times. We muddle through somehow."

Austin cupped Branimir's face in his hands and brushed his thumb over Branimir's bottom lip. "I'm glad you have people who care for you. I think you've added one more to your family."

"I did?" Branimir licked the pad of Austin's thumb.

"Mmm....yes." Austin leaned forward and took Branimir's lips.

The older man opened for him, and he stroked his tongue in and out, imitating the more intimate encounter he looked forward to having soon with Branimir. He moaned as Branimir slid his hands down and squeezed Austin's ass. Wiggling, he straddled Branimir's thighs.

Branimir pulled back. "Don't hurt yourself, honey."

"I'm okay. I'll let you know if something hurts."

He settled into Branimir's embrace as they made out like two teenagers necking on the couch. The only good thing was no parents were going to wander in and catch them.

*   *   *

Branimir climbed up onto the hill behind the barns and stared up at the stars. He had come out there to shift and run, but he didn't feel like it anymore. Austin slept in his bed, causing Branimir's attention to waver back toward the house.

"I think I love him, Til. I think he's the one to join you in my heart." Branimir smiled up into the night sky. "You'd like him. He's just as passionate about horses as you were, and just as talented as you. If I didn't know better, I'd think you were reincarnated into Austin when you died."

Another breeze teased his hair, and again his heart eased. Til's approval, even though he probably imagined it, let him head back to Austin happily.

CHAPTER 4

Branimir stretched as he lay in bed, knowing he should get up, but wondering if he could be lazy for a little bit. He didn't get to sleep in very often. When Til was alive, his partner would take care of the horses sometimes to let Branimir wake up. He rolled over and checked the clock.

Frowning, he realized it would be a few minutes before his alarm went off. What had caused his body to wake up early, even if it was only a few minutes? He inhaled deeply, and the scent of brewing coffee caught his attention. Ah yes, the nectar of the gods to a busy man in the morning.

He climbed out of bed and went to the bathroom. After he finished his morning routine, he dressed and headed downstairs. The smell of bacon and eggs cooking drifted down the hallway, bringing a smile to his face.

"You know, I could get used to having my own personal cook," he said as he strolled into the kitchen.

Austin shot him a grin over his shoulder while standing at the stove. "It's been a few weeks since I practically moved in. I have to do something to earn my keep around here, though the doctor said I could start riding again."

"Really?" Branimir went to the coffeepot and poured out his first cup of the day. Austin had set out the milk and sugar for him.

"Yeah. Only a couple hours to start with, but I can build up from there until I'm riding my normal six or eight hours a day." Austin's movements were graceful as he plated the bacon and eggs before handing it to Branimir. "My hip doesn't hurt at all, and while my ankle's still a little sore, I've ridden with worse injuries."

Branimir brushed a kiss over Austin's cheek. He sat at the table and waited until Austin joined him before he took his first bite. The younger man was moving easier and seemed to be in less pain.

"Shows what country living can do for you. You should consider it instead of your jet set life of a different horse show every weekend." He winked and Austin laughed.

"Right. Like you don't work as hard as I do. You just send others to shows to do the riding for you." Austin cocked his head to the side and studied Branimir. "Why don't you go to more shows yourself?"

Chuckling, Branimir shook his head. "I'm a good rider, but Til was great. He was the face of our business, which worked out because he was a far better rider than me. I'm not fond of crowds, so even when I went to shows with Til, I tended to stay in the barn with the horses while he worked the clients."

"Sounds like you made the perfect couple," Austin commented.

"I don't know about that. We had our arguments, and Til wasn't overly fond of the retraining/rehabilitation part of our business." Branimir leaned forward and laid his hand over Austin's. "Trust me. I haven't put Til on a pedestal and idealized him. I remember all his faults and irritating quirks, as well as all the good times we had."

Austin turned his hand over and entwined their fingers. "I'm not jealous of your relationship with Tilman. I understand he was a huge part of your life, and you shouldn't feel bad for talking about him or anything like that. Actually, I like hearing about your past, and since most of it included Tilman, I can't complain when you mention him."

"Thanks."

Branimir stood and circled the table. He cupped the back of Austin's head and bent to kiss him. Bacon, coffee, and a hint of mint mingled as their tongues dueled. Branimir moaned when Austin palmed his erection through his jeans. He pressed against Austin's hand, matching the rhythmic thrust of his tongue into Austin's mouth.

His balls drew tight to his body and he balanced on the edge of climax. It had been a while, plus he'd been fighting such a strong attraction to Austin without being able to fulfill it because of Austin's injuries. Now the younger man was healed and all the fantasies Branimir had indulged in over the last month could be acted on.

He pulled Austin to his feet, ignoring the clatter of the chair hitting the floor. Encircling Austin's waist, he brought their bodies close enough together, there wasn't an inch of space between them. Austin grabbed Branimir's ass with both hands and they rocked together.

Gasps filled the air as their cocks rubbed against each other. Branimir tipped Austin's head back, trailing kisses over the man's jaw and along his neck to the triangle at the base of his throat. He licked the soft skin there, taking in Austin's salty flavor. He wanted to taste the very essence of Austin, so he eased back a little and dropped to his knees before him.

Austin groaned. "God, I've been dying to feel your lips around my cock since the first time we met."

Branimir leered. "Well, you'll be getting your wish in about a minute or as long as it takes for me to undo your pants."

He struggled with the button and zipper because his hands trembled so much. He eventually achieved his goal and exposed Austin's dick to the morning light. It jutted out from its nest of blond curls, proud and strong. Branimir licked his lips in anticipation of being able to fill his mouth with Austin.

Leaning, he breathed in the musky scent of man and fresh smell of soap left from Austin's morning shower. He ran his tongue from the base of Austin's shaft to the flared head.

"Oh my fucking God," Austin murmured, his hands gripping the sides of Branimir's head.

Smiling inside at Austin's reaction, Branimir pressed the tip of his tongue to Austin's slit and hummed with happiness when Austin shuddered in reaction. He tasted the pre-cum leaking from Austin's cock. It fueled his hunger for more of the man.

A knock on the back door brought them back to reality, and Branimir swore as he shot to his feet.

"Son-of-a-bitch," he muttered, adjusting himself in his constricting jeans before turning to go answer the door.

"My sentiments exactly," Austin agreed.

Branimir opened the door to find Lissa standing there. "What do you need, Lissa?"

"Sorry to bother you before you get down to the barn, but that mare you brought in freaked out. She was out in the paddock when Tomas went to bring Sparky in. The farrier's here to do the horses' shoes and they went in with her, since Sparky is now in the same paddock."

"Damn." Branimir glanced around at Austin. "I have to get out to the barn. Mary's Gospel seems to have taken exception to Tomas' entry into her space."

"And she wasn't happy about him taking Sparky with him," Lissa pointed out.

"Really?" Austin picked up his plate and took it to the sink. "I want to come with you."

"Come down when you're ready." Branimir followed Lissa, shaking his head. "I should have told everyone to stay out of Mary's paddock. She's not ready to trust anyone. I'm happy she takes to Sparky so well."

"Don't worry, boss. Tomas should've known better. He's been working here for a couple of years now. He knows how abused horses get territorial." Lissa sighed.

"Is he all right?"

"Oh, yes. Sparky actually blocked her, so she couldn't do anything except scare him a little."

Branimir went into the barn where Sparky stood in the aisle way. Digs, his stable manager, circled around the thoroughbred. The gelding snorted as Branimir walked up to him. He stroked his hand over Sparky's nose.

"How's he doing?"

"Just a scratch and a bruise. He's a tough old bird and has probably had worse when he was racing." Digs chuckled and patted Sparky's shoulder. "I'll doctor up the scratch and put him in his stall for the day."

"Thanks. I'm going out to see if Mary'll let me close."

"Good way to start a morning, huh?" Digs grinned as Branimir nodded and walked out toward the paddock where Mary paced along the fence line.

Branimir sensed, rather than saw, Austin's arrival at the barn when he approached the mare.

"Be careful," Austin said loudly enough for Branimir to hear, but not so loud he startled Mary.

Waving his hand, Branimir murmured, "It's all right, pretty lady. I'm not here to hurt you or invade your space."

Stopping, Mary whinnied, and Sparky answered. Once the gelding responded, the mare paced along the fence, keeping her eyes on Branimir. Her coat was sweaty and she was breathing heavily, but she wasn't as upset as she had been when she arrived a month ago. Branimir had worked to get her to accept his presence around her.

He waited, knowing she would come around. Finally, ten minutes

39

later, she halted next to him with the fence separating them.

"That's it. You know my voice and smell. I won't hurt you, honey. Sparky's fine. Tomas wasn't going to do anything to him."

The cadence of his voice was soothed her, but she still wasn't willing to let him close. He braced his elbows on the top rail, humming softly. Austin eased up next to him as Mary nickered.

"You recognize him, don't you, sweetheart?" Branimir bumped shoulders with Austin. "He brought you food and gave you a safe place to heal. Austin's never done anything to scare you."

His every gesture was slow and easy as he encircled Austin's waist with his arm. Mary slid closer as well, her nose reaching out toward Branimir.

"Not that I'm complaining, but why are you cuddling with me in the middle of your farm?" Austin rested his head on Branimir's shoulder.

"Because she associates our separate smells as good. We haven't done anything bad to her or hurt her. Standing and rubbing against each other, we're sharing our scents and they're mingling for her." Branimir nuzzled Austin's hair. "Besides I actually like this."

Austin chuckled and pressed tighter to him. "So do I."

Branimir continued to talk to Mary, chatting about nothing and allowing the mare to approach them. Another ten minutes and Mary's Gospel stood right next to them, offering up her neck and shoulder for them to pet.

He smiled as Austin scratched her neck and her skin twitched. It was good for Mary to get used to having Austin around her. They would be spending time with each other once Branimir got her mentally strong enough to deal with shows and a rider.

Austin's warm body resting against his settled something inside Branimir he hadn't known was restless. He loved Austin's freshly showered smell and the underlying scent of man. He trailed kisses along Austin's jaw, and Austin dropped his head, giving Branimir more access to his throat.

Mary bumped Branimir's arm with her nose, and he laughed as their heads smacked together slightly.

"I'm not sure what she's trying to say, but in a way she's right. This isn't the best place for us to make out." Branimir sighed and stepped away.

"Ah, well, I guess we'll have to pick this up later." Austin winked. "Hey, can I work Buster? My cousin's coming down with his client, and I wanted to ride the gelding. Also, there are a few others I'd like to try. I'm still looking for a mount for my niece and I might end up finding a new mount for myself."

"Don't you think you have enough horses?" Branimir patted Mary's neck before walking away.

"Shouldn't you spend more time with her?" Austin did the same.

"No. I think we've spent enough time with her. She's stressed enough because of Tomas and Sparky. I walk away, and she relaxes. It's called building trust with Mary. Maybe next time she lets me touch her head."

Austin looked thoughtful as they made their way to the second barn. Branimir waved Lissa over.

"Don't worry about Mary. She's doing fine, but we should put Sparky back out with her as soon as possible. She feels safer with him there."

"Sure, boss."

"Oh, and can you saddle Buster for me? Mr. Spellsin wants to work him out a little. Also, why don't you bring out Spots? I'd like to get on her and see how she's been progressing." Branimir squeezed Lissa's shoulder. "You're doing a good job working with her."

She laughed. "I know, but it never hurts to have the boss double-check my work. Besides, you're the best rider here. Well, you were until Spellsin showed up."

After she walked away, Austin leaned forward and whispered in Branimir's ear, "Just wait until you see how I can ride you later on."

"Fuck me," Branimir uttered under his breath.

"Oh, that'll happen as well." Austin chuckled.

*   *   *

Night fell and Austin put the finishing touches on dinner while Branimir helped his stable hands bed the horses for the night. Austin had offered to assist, but Branimir sent him in because he was still healing and Branimir didn't want Austin to reinjure anything.

He set the table and checked the steaks once more before he opened the bottle of wine. Austin wiped his palms on his jeans as he looked around the dining room. Did he forget anything? Was it too much or too obvious what he was trying to do?

"Something smells good," Branimir commented as he walked into the mudroom.

"You had some steaks thawed out in the refrigerator, so I thought

I'd cook them up before they go bad." He grinned as Branimir padded up to him in his socks.

Branimir slid his hand into the curls at the nape of Austin's neck, drawing him close for a quick kiss. "Do I have time for a shower? I won't take long."

Austin thought about it and nodded. "Yeah. The steaks need about five more minutes as does the asparagus."

"Great. I'll be right back."

After ogling Branimir's ass, Austin went back into the kitchen to plate the food. By the time he got all of it to the table, Branimir was coming downstairs. They met in the dining room, and Branimir poured them each a glass of wine. They sat and Branimir held up his glass.

"A toast to new beginnings and new relationships."

"I'll toast to that." Austin touched his glass to Branimir's and took a sip. "Everyone settled in for the night?"

Branimir nodded. "Yeah. Mary's calmed down...being next to Sparky helps. He's fine and can go back out in the paddock with her tomorrow."

"Good. I'd have felt bad if she'd injured him."

"I love this wine." Branimir glanced at his glass. "It actually happened to be one of Til's favorites."

Austin tensed. "I'm sorry. I found it in the wine cellar and I knew it would go with the steak."

"Don't worry. I'm not going to freak out or anything. Til was the wine drinker in the family. I'm more of a beer guy when I feel like drinking." Branimir grinned.

"Well, Tilman had good taste. There were some good wines down there." Austin took a bite of his steak and moaned. "Damn, that's good, even if I say so myself."

Branimir grunted because his mouth was full of steak. They settled down to finish the meal. When Branimir finished, he leaned back and patted his stomach.

"I haven't eaten that well in a long time. It's hard to cook for one sometimes and I don't usually have people over." Branimir frowned. "Maybe I should do that more often. Kind of lost touch with the friends Til and I had."

Austin stood and carried their plates to the kitchen to put in the sink. He grabbed the cookies he'd baked earlier, along with two glasses of milk. He carried them out toward the dining room, but Branimir met him in the hallway.

"Why don't we have dessert in the living room?"

Branimir took the cookies from him and led the way into the other room. Austin curled on the couch and his heart skipped a beat when Branimir joined him, encircling his shoulders with an arm to pull him closer.

He snuggled into Branimir's side, breathing in the clean scent from Branimir's shower, yet there still was an underlying smell of horse. It didn't bother Austin since he loved horses.

"Tell me a secret no one else knows about you," he said, then amended it. "No one else except for Tilman. I'm sure you didn't have any secrets from him."

Branimir stayed silent for a little while, and Austin wondered if there had been secrets between the two lovers. The funny thing was Austin never got the feeling Branimir idealized his relationship with Tilman. When Branimir talked about his late lover, it sounded like Branimir did love the man and missed him, but he didn't pine for his lost partner.

It was hard to tell why Branimir hadn't had a serious relationship after Til died. It'd been five years and Branimir admitted he hadn't been with anyone for any length of time. Had it simply been because Tilman was Branimir's soul mate or was it just that Branimir was too busy with other things to worry about his personal life?

"I hate the dark," Branimir confessed.

Austin eased back slightly and stared at Branimir. "Seriously? Tilman didn't know that?"

"No. It never really mattered. I do all right when there's someone with me, but when I'm alone, I usually have a small light on." Branimir looked uncomfortable.

"I needed a nightlight until I was, like, sixteen." Austin smiled. "You know what my secret is. I can't whistle."

Branimir chuckled. "I'm not sure why you'd keep that a secret, but thanks for sharing. I'll still sleep with you, even though you can't whistle during sex."

They laughed until Austin met Branimir's gaze, and they came together hard, teeth clacking as they kissed. He threaded his fingers through Branimir's hair and moaned low in his throat as Branimir grabbed his ass. Wiggling and squirming, he straddled Branimir's lap.

He ground his erection into Branimir's, and their groans mingled. He dropped his head back and kept rocking their groins together. Branimir encouraged the rhythm until panting filled the room. Sweat dripped down his cheeks, and Austin leaned forward to nip Branimir's neck.

"You're so beautiful," he murmured as he nibbled along Branimir's throat, taking little bites as he went.

"As are you." Branimir squeezed Austin's ass, running his finger along the seam of Austin's jeans and pressing just a little against Austin's hole.

The pressure from Branimir's finger made Austin want more. He reached down and opened his pants, revealing his cock. Branimir caught on to what Austin was doing, so he undid his own jeans and brought their naked shafts together.

"Holy shit!"

The heat of Branimir's skin, along with the strength of his fingers wrapped around his own shaft, drove Austin closer to the edge. He thrust, fucking Branimir's hand, letting their pre-cum ease the friction, but only slightly. There was a little bite of pain to the hand job.

"I'm coming," he warned.

"I'm right with you."

Within seconds, warm cum spilled from him, coating their cocks and Branimir's hand. When his last drop squirted out, Branimir came, adding his own to Austin's. As his climax faded away, he fell forward onto Branimir's chest.

"Wow. I needed that," he muttered.

"So did I, but I want in your ass." Branimir patted his butt before gathering him close and standing. "Let's go take a shower and see where we can go from there."

"Sounds great to me."

He wrapped his legs around Branimir's waist and rested his head on Branimir's shoulder, letting his lover carry him upstairs. He marveled at how strong Branimir was, considering Austin wasn't a lightweight, but Branimir wasn't out of breath when he hit the top of the stairs.

They moved down the hallway to the bathroom, where Branimir set Austin on the counter before turning on the shower. Austin sat there for a moment, watching his lover strip. It shouldn't have been erotic because Branimir wasn't trying to be. He unbuttoned and removed each piece of clothing without even looking at Austin.

When Branimir revealed his upper body, Austin gasped. Scars marred his chest and back like he'd been in a lot of fights. One scar looked more like a horse attacked him. Austin jumped to his feet and went over to run his fingers over the jagged line.

"Wow, that had to hurt," he commented.

Branimir stiffened, but didn't pull away. "It did."

"How did it happen? I can't see you not paying close enough attention to let a horse nail you like that." Austin noticed how tense Branimir appeared as he continued to trace the old wound.

"Yeah, well, I wasn't really expecting it from this particular horse. He'd never shown any signs of aggression toward me before, but I guess it just goes to show you can't get distracted, even around a horse you trust."

Austin studied Branimir, something in the man's voice telling Austin there was more to the story. Yet the way Branimir turned away from him told Austin that Branimir didn't want to talk about it.

"Looks like you had quite a few run-ins with crazy animals." He whispered a caress over Branimir's chest, pausing to tweak his nipple.

Branimir hissed and reached for Austin's pants. "You need to get naked, and we need to get wet before all the hot water is gone."

Austin chuckled as he ripped his clothes off and crowded Branimir into the shower stall. He inhaled sharply as the wet fell over Branimir's body, outlining all those wonderful muscles and tanned skin. The man must sunbathe in the nude because there wasn't a tan line anywhere. Austin almost swallowed his tongue at the thought of Branimir lying on the grass out under the sun. God, he hoped he got to see it just once before he had to leave.

"Shit," he muttered as he soaped up his hands and grasped Branimir's cock with them. He pumped, while Branimir dropped his head back and groaned.

"What's wrong?"

He could tell Branimir had a hard time focusing on what Austin said and Austin wanted it that way.

"Nothing…just remembered something."

Austin pushed the thought of leaving out of his head. He didn't have to go for another month and, after that, he'd figure out how to get back to Branimir and his farm as often as possible. Long distance relationships were hard on couples, but luckily, he had the money to make it work, even if he had to fly back to Branimir every week.

What did that say about his feelings for the man? They'd only spent time together for the past month or so, and while he did know Branimir better than when he'd arrived, there were still lots of things he didn't know about the man.

Branimir grabbed Austin's shoulders and brought their mouths together, quite effectively stopping Austin from thinking about anything except the feel of Branimir's thick cock in his hand.

Their tongues competed for dominance as Branimir pushed Austin up against the cool tiles. He grunted at the coldness on his back, but his chills disappeared when Branimir slid his hands down to grip his ass with strong fingers.

"Oh, fuck." He moaned, arching into Branimir's solid body. His own grip on Branimir's cock tightened, but his mind short-circuited at the touch of Branimir's fingers to his hole.

"You want something," Branimir murmured, tongue trailing over the curves of Austin's ear.

"God, yes. I want you inside me. You're gonna make me feel you for days." His eyes rolled at the thought of Branimir's larger than average cock fucking his hole.

Branimir growled low in his throat before pressing closer to Austin and nipping the side of Austin's neck. Austin exhaled loudly and turned to brace his hands against the wall, tilting his ass out in a blatant offer. He jumped when Branimir slapped his butt.

"Don't move. I'll be right back."

Austin rested his forehead on the tiles and closed his eyes, calming his breathing so he didn't hyperventilate. At what point had his entire focus narrowed down to the shower stall and the man about to fuck him? Nothing else mattered except getting Branimir's dick in his ass.

He grunted when a slick finger rubbed over his hole lightly before breaching it. Closing his eyes, he concentrated on relaxing his muscles. Branimir buried his finger as deep as it could go into Austin, and they both grunted. Within minutes, Branimir had four fingers stretching Austin, getting him ready for Branimir's thick shaft.

"I'm ready, Branimir. I want you inside me right now," Austin demanded.

Branimir chuckled and eased his fingers out, drawing a mumbled protest from Austin. "Can't have it both ways, sweetheart. It'd take far more lube for you to be able to deal with all my fingers and my cock. It'd be like me fucking you with my fist."

Austin almost came as the image of Branimir's hand buried in his ass popped up in his mind. "Oh my God!"

"Hush, honey." Branimir soothed Austin by stroking his hand over Austin's back. "That's something to think about later. Right now, I want to shove my dick into you as hard as I can until you're screaming my name."

"Do it."

He dropped his head again and shut his eyes, admiring Branimir's controlled power as his lover thrust slowly, inch by hot inch. He was panting by the time Branimir stopped, his pubic hair scratching Austin's butt.

"Are you okay?"

Austin thought for a moment, evaluating every atom in his body. Was he okay? He hummed and angled his hips, drawing Branimir in farther. Oh yeah, he felt great.

"Yeah. I'm fine. Get moving, stud."

Branimir froze, and Austin wondered what he'd said. He clenched his inner muscles, dragging a groan from Branimir. That was all the man need, Austin guessed, considering how quickly Branimir started fucking his ass. Hard and fast, just like Austin wanted at that moment.

He grunted and jerked as Branimir nailed his gland with each stroke in and out. Stars burst before his eyes when Branimir leaned forward and bit the spot where his neck and shoulder met.

"Branimir," Austin screamed.

Without even being touched, Austin came, spilling his cum all over the shower wall and floor. He massaged Branimir's cock, doing his best to break the man's control. It worked.

One. Two. On the third deep shove inside, Branimir froze and shouted Austin's name, while filling the condom he wore. His hands gripped Austin's hips, and they would leave behind bruises, but Austin didn't care. He barely acknowledged it when Branimir slid out and somehow managed to get them cleaned up, out of the shower, and into bed without a mishap, considering how useless Austin was.

They snuggled together under the blankets in Branimir's bed, and Austin thought about how sexy Branimir made him feel, but also how much love he felt in every touch. It was crazy, of course, because no one falls in love so quickly. Austin sighed and wiggled to get closer to Branimir. He'd worry about all that in the morning. Right now, he wanted to sleep in the arms of his lover and absorb his warmth.

CHAPTER 5

Branimir lifted his head and sniffed the air. A storm was coming. He needed to get back to the house and bed before Austin woke up and noticed him missing. He wasn't ready for Austin to know his secret. Snorting, Branimir whirled on his hind legs and trotted back down the trail toward the barn.

Even though he lived with and loved Til for fifteen years, he'd never once thought about telling his lover his secret. He explained his midnight runs as restlessness and homesickness. Til never questioned him deeper, letting him keep his true nature hidden. Would he ever have revealed himself to Til? He didn't know and it wasn't worth wasting the energy thinking about it.

The night air drifted around him and danced in his nose as he stretched his long legs into a gallop. He loved running, and it was one of the things he missed not being in Montana. There had been a lot of space for him to run without worrying whether he'd run into anyone or not. Fewer people around meant less people to notice a stray horse.

The barns came into sight and he sped up. Branimir could feel the electricity of the storm building. He hated being out in thunderstorms or rain showers of any kind. He ducked into the barn where he'd left his clothes when he shifted. He walked into a stall before taking a deep breath and letting go of his horse.

Changing from one shape to another wasn't painful. It was exhausting and he'd fall right to sleep as soon as his head hit the pillow. If anyone ever asked him what it was like, he'd describe it as shedding a coat and putting on a different one. Both were comfortable with age and use. Once he felt the last of the horse slip from him, he stretched and opened his eyes.

Blinking, he waited until his eyesight adjusted again. It was weird going from the eyes of a prey animal to those of a predator. That whole eyes-on-the-sides-of-his-head to the usual situation of eyes in the center of his face. When he knew he could walk without stumbling or staggering, he dressed and headed through the barn out to the house.

After entering, Branimir went to the kitchen and grabbed a glass of water. Shifting made him hungry as well, but he didn't like to eat in the middle of the night, so he'd settle for a larger than usual breakfast in the morning. He set the glass in the sink with a gentle clink before making his way upstairs to his bedroom where Austin slept.

Austin hadn't moved, except to roll over on his side facing away from the door. Standing there, Branimir stared down at the younger man with a faint smile. Young, gorgeous, rich and amazingly talented, Austin Spellsin had every reason to be arrogant and selfish. Yet Branimir had never seen or heard of Austin treating anyone badly. It was apparent from the way he took care of his horses how much he loved them and respected them. The animals did their best to perform for him, but without being fearful of his anger.

More than anything, Branimir studied how the horses reacted to people. They had a much clearer view of humans and a natural instinct as to who would hurt them and who would treat them well. So far he hadn't seen any of the horses act badly around him, except for Mary's Gospel.

She didn't really count because her view of humans had been warped by years of abuse by them. The mare was slowly coming around with each new day. Branimir didn't push her to accept him. He understood years of abuse couldn't be stripped away in a few hours. He was willing to take his time helping her heal.

Branimir stripped and slipped back under the covers, curling around Austin with a soft sigh.

Austin shifted slightly and murmured, "Where did you go? Are the mares okay?"

"Yes. Just needed to use the bathroom," he replied.

"Okay."

Austin's body relaxed into his arms, and Branimir closed his eyes, allowing his muscles to ease as the tension drained from him. At times, it was hard running the farm alone. It had been their dream for so long and without Til, Branimir sometimes felt fate or God was cheating him. Horses weren't solitary creatures. They were meant to be part of a herd, even if the herd consisted of only two animals. Even after being driven from the family ranch, Branimir had sought out others to befriend and make his herd.

When Til died, Branimir allowed their circle of friends to drift away, leaving him alone without a herd to call his own. He admitted it was his own fault. They would have stuck around, but they were mostly Til's friends who'd accepted Branimir into their circle because Til loved him. He'd left all of his friends behind in Montana when he followed Til home to Kentucky.

He buried his face in the curls at the base of Austin's neck and breathed in the scent of sweat and horses with an underlying layer of pure Austin. How could a man smell expensive? It wasn't the cologne Austin used because Branimir recognized it as the same kind Til had used. No, the scent he inhaled smelled of confidence. Austin knew his place in the world and that assurance turned Branimir on. It was the same thing he'd found most attractive about Til. They knew where they belonged in the grand scheme of things.

Branimir struggled every day to find the place he felt most at home. The farm was the closest spot at the moment, along with being wrapped around Austin and lying in his bed. Branimir would accept that for right now and worry about the rest of it later. No point in getting upset over it.

Wiggling a little, he brought Austin closer to him and closed his eyes. Nelson, Austin's cousin, had called earlier in the day to let them know he would be arriving in the morning with his client to look at some horses. Branimir smiled and let sleep overcome him.

*   *   *

Watching Austin ride Buster around the arena, Branimir admired how Austin made the gelding look better than the horse really was. Buster still wasn't as flexible as needed to be a Grand Prix horse, but he would always be a good Intermediate horse.

"The gelding looks good. Do you think Clarissa could try him next?" Nelson asked as he joined Branimir at the rail.

"Sure." He whistled, grabbing Austin's attention. When his lover glanced at him, he waved. "Bring Buster over. Clarissa wants to ride him."

Austin nodded and turned the gelding in their direction. They arrived at the rail just as Clarissa appeared with her own tack. They switched everything out, and Branimir gave her a leg up.

He climbed back through the fence and handed Austin's tack off to Lissa. Nelson called out movements for Clarissa to try, testing her communication with the horse.

"They look good together," Austin commented.

"Clarissa's a good rider, but she's not interested in moving up to the Grand Prix level. I think Buster's a good fit for her," Nelson agreed.

Branimir smiled as Austin and Nelson began talking about some of the other horses in Branimir's barn. Nelson and his client had shown up early in the morning and were going to stay a couple days, just to check out a few others. Nelson was always looking for good horses to pair up with his long list of clients. Plus he'd decided to help Austin look for a mount for Austin's niece.

He let them continue chatting while he wandered off. It was time to see about putting a bridle on Mary. He'd succeeded the other day in getting her to accept a saddle. She still didn't like his hands around her head, but without too much stress, maybe they could try the bridle today. The mare wasn't ready for a rider yet. Branimir decided when she was, he'd like Austin be the first to ride her. It would build a lot of trust between them.

Stopping in front of Mary's stall, he studied the rangy chestnut mare. Mary stood, eyeing him as well. She'd gotten used to his scent and accepted him as the herd stallion, but his human smell confused her at times. He let her take a few minutes to mingle the two in her brain.

After lifting her halter from the hook, along with a lead rope, he entered her stall and got the halter on without any problem. She'd learned to trust him with those objects. He led her out into the aisle way and attached the crossties to her halter.

"This Austin's mare?"

Branimir glanced up to see Nelson standing a few feet away. Mary snorted when she saw him, but didn't shy or retreat from him. She'd learned not every human would hurt her. It didn't mean she trusted easily or quickly. It still took her time to allow someone new to touch her. Branimir stroked her neck and murmured to her before grabbing her brush to groom her.

"Yes. This is Mary's Gospel."

"Damn it. It's just not fair. The man always has the best luck." Nelson circled her, keeping clear of her hind legs and making sure not to touch her. "I only got to see pictures of her right after he got her. God, if Billings had been in front of me, I'd probably would have beat him within an inch of his life."

Nelson's anger echoed Branimir's when he thought of what Billings had done to the mare.

"Yeah, I know what you mean. The rest of his horses were just as bad off. The ASPCA came in and seized them. I've kept track of them all and they've been moving on to new homes at a good pace. I think they're all due for a great life soon." Branimir cleaned out her hooves and gave her a carrot when he finished.

"Glad to hear it. So how's she doing? She's looking better than she did."

Branimir smiled. "Mary's doing marvelous. I got a saddle on her a couple of days ago and now I'm thinking it's time for the bridle. She's not ready for a rider yet. I want her to put several more pounds on before I do that. Hey, can you grab that bridle for me?"

He unhooked one of the ties before slipping the reins over Mary's head to rest on her neck. After unclipping the other side, he let the halter go and slid the bridle on. Mary tensed, but she let him slip the bridle on. It was a bitless version because Branimir knew the metal would hurt her mouth. He fastened the buckles and led her from the barn to the outdoor arena. There weren't any riders out there at the moment. Branimir glanced over at Nelson, who followed with the saddle.

"Oh, Austin took Clarissa out for a ride on the trails. He said you wouldn't mind."

"Nah. Buster's a good trail horse. He shouldn't give her any trouble." Branimir brought Mary into the arena, leaving the gate open for Nelson.

He left the reins over her neck, twisting them and sliding the throatlatch strap thru them. Not knowing how Mary would react to the blanket or the saddle, he didn't want to tie her to anything. It helped to insure she didn't injure herself or someone else if she freaked out.

Mary stood there, her head up and gaze curious as Branimir took the blanket from Nelson. He held it up for her to sniff before rubbing it along her neck. Her skin twitched, but she didn't shy away from it. She didn't seem to have bad memories of blankets. He settled it on her back up over her withers and tugging back until it sat just right. He didn't want any hair twisted under it or any lumps.

Branimir waited a few minutes until Mary dropped her head and chewed, showing how relaxed she'd become.

"That's a good sign," Nelson muttered.

"Yep. Now for the saddle."

Branimir took it from Nelson and walked up to Mary, letting her sniff it all over. Again, no negative reaction, so he stepped to the side and carefully lowered the saddle onto her back. She tensed, but didn't kick out or try to buck it off. He tightened the girth and gathered her reins to walk her around the arena.

At first, Mary's Gospel moved with tension, making her stride short and choppy. Branimir didn't rush her, and ten minutes later, she walked confidently beside him, unconcerned about the saddle or the bridle. Another ten minutes and Branimir called it quits.

He wasn't interested in pushing her too far too fast. She'd been doing well with each step. Nelson helped him and by the time they released the mare in her paddock, Austin and Clarissa were back.

*   *   *

"When're you heading back out? I know there are a couple of shows coming up, plus Hampton's in another couple of weeks." Nelson bumped his shoulder against Austin's as he joined him at the stove.

"I have an appointment with my doctor next week. Once I get the all-clear, I'll be hitting the shows again. I've been back to the farm often enough to make sure everything is running well without my constant presence." Austin stirred the beans sautéing in a pan. "I'll admit it's been nice just to ride horses and not worry about owners. Which shows are the best to expose our horses to the right people."

"Comes with running your own barn, cousin. That's why I chose not to run a barn, but to be a broker and find horses for clients." Nelson smiled at him. "Do you want me to set the table?"

"Yeah. Branimir and Clarissa should be in soon. What were they doing anyway?" Austin checked the chicken in the oven and saw it was almost done.

Nelson got the plates and silverware out. "Branimir was showing her the foals. He's got a nice breeding program here. The whole operation is pretty impressive."

Austin nodded. "It is and especially since he's doing it with throwaway horses. Just goes to show every horse should be given a chance to achieve its potential."

"Glad you feel that way," Branimir said as he walked into the kitchen with Clarissa.

"Were you suitably impressed with the babies?" Nelson gestured to the wine open on the counter. "Would you like a glass?"

Clarissa nodded. "They were adorable. I love the young ones. So many possibilities and untrained enthusiasm. I'm going to wash up, but I'd love some wine."

Austin watched the petite brunette leave and grinned at Branimir. His lover shook his head.

"She might be an amateur rider, but she knows horses. It was almost like having my dad around, asking me every possible question about them." Branimir washed his hands in the sink and breathed deeply as he dried them on a towel. "It smells really good. I'm going to go into withdrawal when you leave."

"You're a good cook yourself. You need to start asking people over. It'll give you an excuse to cook." Austin plated the food and carried it to the table.

The men waited until Clarissa returned before sitting and starting to eat. The conversation centered on horses and competitions. Branimir didn't have much to say on the shows. Austin knew he only went to them to drum up business and he didn't really enjoy showing. An idea popped into his head.

"I know you don't really like going to shows," he commented to Branimir.

"It was always what Til liked doing the most. He enjoyed schmoozing people and dealing with all the politics involved. I want to show the horses off to their best, but I don't enjoy the crowds and shit." Branimir leaned back in his chair, resting his hands on his stomach.

Austin, Nelson, and Clarissa laughed.

"I understand, so I want to propose a deal. You send the horses you want prospective buyers to have a chance to look at to me. I'll trailer them to the shows and have some of my riders show them for you. You aren't away from the farm and more people will get the opportunity to see your product."

"What do you get out of this deal?" Branimir studied him with an amused tilt to his lips.

"The most important thing is I get to see you more often. Not that I really needed to have an excuse, but it helps that we both get something out of it. Having more mounts available for my clients to ride helps me out as well. They get more experience and I don't have to pay for the horse's feed and board. Since they won't be spending all their time with us." He snorted. "Of course, with the quality of horses you have here, I'm going to have to curb the urge to keep all of them."

Nelson pushed his plate away from him and rested his elbows on the table. "It would be a good partnership. Also, I'd be better able to get my clients to the shows to check out your horses instead of traveling here."

Branimir pursed his lips. "I'd have to think about it and go over the numbers with you to make sure it won't be cost-prohibitive for either of us. I do like the idea of not having to go to shows and I know I can trust you with my horses."

"Take as much time as you want." Austin stood and took a stack of plates to the sink.

Branimir shooed them out of the kitchen. "I'll clean up while you all relax in the living room."

Austin led the others out of the room. He flopped onto the couch with a sigh, while Nelson and Clarissa took the chairs across from him.

"I've always heard good things about this place at all the shows. People know he's the one to call when there are horses in trouble. Even if he doesn't take them himself, he knows who to call to help out." Clarissa sighed. "I'm definitely interested in Buster. He and I will burn up the shows once we've been together for a little while."

"You're a good fit. You'll push him without asking him to do things he can't accomplish. That's what he needs." Austin sipped his wine.

"I think a little bit of Branimir's grasp of horse mentality has rubbed off on you," Nelson pointed out with a smile.

"It's almost like he can read their minds at times. He knows when they're going to freak out. He knows just how far to push them and he stops right before it gets to be too much. I've never seen anyone train the way he does."

Branimir walked in and sat next to him. "You do this for as long as I have, you get a feel for how they think. It's as simple as that."

Yet Austin had the feeling, after watching Branimir work for over a month, there was more to Branimir's abilities than simple experience.

They talked for a few more hours about horses and shows, even people they knew and Branimir had run into at certain horse places. It felt comfortable and like home, which sort of freaked Austin out a little. It shouldn't be this easy, falling into a routine like he and Branimir were already partners. Life wasn't that simple.

After Nelson and Clarissa went up to bed, Austin and Branimir went down to the barns to check on the horses one last time. Austin stopped in front of Mary's stall, and to his happy surprise, Mary stuck out her nose to greet him. It was the first time the mare had ever made the first move toward him. Usually it took him several minutes to convince her to approach him. He stroked his hand over her soft nose.

"How are you doing, sweetheart? Are you enjoying your luxurious accommodations?" He pulled pieces of apple from his pocket to feed Mary a bedtime snack.

"Only the best for our visitors." Branimir joined him and wrapped an arm around his waist.

Austin rested back against Branimir's solid body. "When she's ready to come to my barn, she's going to be very upset. My place isn't bad, but not nearly as nice as yours."

"I'm sure she'll love her stall in your barn as much as she likes it here. Of course, she might miss Sparky." Branimir nodded at the gelding in the stall next to Mary's. "If you have the space, you might want to consider taking Sparky with you. Some horses need a particular friend to keep them relaxed."

"Are you trying to get me to buy Sparky?" Austin chuckled.

Branimir shook his head. "I'd let you take him for free because he really isn't good for anything except a trail ride or a leisurely ride around the arena. If you had little kids who wanted to learn how to ride, Sparky would be the perfect mount for them."

Austin smiled, but didn't say anything. He'd already decided to see if he could take Sparky with them when they left. Mary had grown attached to the gelding, and Austin didn't want her to become anxious in a new place. He could find something for Sparky to do beside eat his fool head off.

Austin got a lot of requests for riding lessons for younger riders. Maybe Branimir was right and he could give lessons. He'd have to give it more thought and see if he could get some more retired horses from Branimir.

A shiver chased its way down his spine as Branimir nuzzled his jaw. He tilted his head, giving his lover more access to his skin. He pressed back into Branimir, rubbing his ass against Branimir's groin. Branimir slid one hand down to cup Austin's jean-covered cock, while the other swept up under Austin's shirt to tease his nipples.

"Maybe we should take this back inside," he whispered.

"Oh, I have a better idea."

He pushed away his disappointment as Branimir stepped away from him. He patted Mary on the nose before he followed the older man down the aisle to the tack room. As he entered, he spotted Branimir pulling several blankets from one of the trunks against the wall.

"Come with me," Branimir ordered, and Austin snorted quietly. "Please, will you come with me?"

Branimir held out his hand, and Austin took it. They wandered down the trail to where it branched off. Taking the left branch, they ended up in a small clearing with a pond. Austin crouched beside the water and dangled his fingers in the cool liquid.

"This is nice." He glanced behind him to see Branimir spreading the blankets.

Austin's heart skipped a beat when Branimir knelt on them and held out his hand.

"Will you join me?"

What could Austin say? He pushed to his feet and strolled to the edge of the fabric. Austin smiled at Branimir as he grabbed the hem of his T-shirt and tugged it over his head. He let it drop from his fingers before reaching for the button on his jeans.

Branimir scooted across the ground and grabbed Austin's hands. "Let me do it."

"All right."

He freed his hand from Branimir's and ran his fingers through Branimir's silver-streaked hair. They shared another smile, while Branimir stripped Austin's clothes off. Austin lay back, resting on his elbows.

"I'm not the only one getting naked here, am I?" He winked.

"No, honey."

Branimir surged to his feet, and Austin's mouth went dry as each inch of tanned skin and well-defined muscles was revealed. All of it for him to enjoy and lick. He couldn't wait. He sat up and crooked a finger in Branimir's direction.

"Come here."

Dropping to his knees, Branimir crawled over to him and ended up straddling Austin's body. Their lips met in a hard kiss, and Austin wrapped one of his hands around Branimir's cock. He invaded Branimir's mouth with his tongue and stroked along it, tempting and teasing Branimir.

He moaned as Branimir pulled back slightly to nibble along Austin's chin and down his neck to suck his nipple. He arched his back, managing to pump Branimir's cock the entire time.

"Wait." He pushed at Branimir's shoulders.

His lover pulled back and raised an eyebrow at him. Austin drew a circle with his finger. "Why don't you turn around and we can have some fun?"

Branimir's eyes blazed with lust as he quickly turned to straddle Austin's head, bringing his cock closer to Austin's mouth. He licked a line from the base of Branimir's shaft to the tip. He pressed into the slit, drawing a groan from Branimir.

When Branimir swallowed Austin's cock down, Austin barely managed to stop from shoving as deep into Branimir's mouth as he could. Once his mind started working again, he began sucking. They moved together, using tongue and lips. Austin fondled Branimir's balls, tugging and massaging them, while he sucked as much of Branimir's shaft as he could. He couldn't take the whole thing in without choking himself.

Branimir tapped his hip, alerting him, and he hummed softly. Salty cum coated his tongue as he drank down Branimir's climax. He grunted and lifted his hips, spilling his own cum into his lover's mouth.

After they finished, they took a quick dip in the pond to rinse off and snuggled under the blanket for a little while before heading back to the house. Not a word was spoken and neither man felt the need to say anything.

CHAPTER 6

Branimir finished grooming Mary and fed her a few carrots before letting her out into her paddock. She whinnied and took off toward Sparky, who stood in the far corner under the large oak shading the corners of four paddocks. He grinned at their enthusiastic greeting. By the way they were acting, he would have thought Mary had been gone for weeks instead of the two hours Branimir had ridden her.

He went back into the barn and packed up her grooming box, returning it to the trunk in front of her stall. Glancing at his watch, he nodded. He had enough time to call Austin before his first lesson of the afternoon showed.

After shutting the door of his office, he settled in his chair and pulled out his cell phone. Branimir dialed Austin's number and leaned back, propping his feet on his desk.

"Hey there." Austin sounded happy.

"Hello, honey. How's the show life treating you?"

"Good so far. It'll take a few more classes to get back into the swing of things, but I'm healthy and that's the important part." Austin laughed. "So to what do I owe the pleasure of your call?"

"I can't just call my boyfriend up in the middle of the day to say hi?" he asked, teasing a little, but also a bit nervous because it was the first time he'd ever called Austin his boyfriend.

Silence filled the air between them for a moment and he realized he'd surprised Austin with the endearment. He shifted uneasily in the chair. Had he moved too fast? Was Austin not ready for their

59

relationship to be as serious as that? Maybe Austin thought once he left, they would just be fuck buddies.

"Wow…does it make me sound weird if I tell you I'm dancing around the barn, frigging excited as hell that you called me your boyfriend?" Austin sounded breathless.

Branimir released his breath. "Doesn't sound weird at all, sweetheart. I have to admit it kind of slipped out, then I panicked about how you were going to react."

Their mirth mingled together as their relief filled them. Branimir rested his head against the chair, staring up at the ceiling of the barn.

"You do know you can call me any time you want, right? Unless I'm in the middle of a class or something, I'll always answer."

"Same here." Branimir sighed. "I wanted to hear your voice, but I also wanted to let you know Mary's ready for you. If you have some free time to come back, I'd like to have you spend some time with her while I'm around."

"Wow. I've only been gone two weeks and you've gotten her ready for me to ride. That's awesome."

Austin's excitement and praise touched Branimir deep inside. It had been quite a few years since he'd let anyone's admiration of him matter so much.

"It wasn't that hard once I put a saddle on her. We worked on helping her get beyond the memories of the past. She knows both of us, and we've never hurt her or forced her to do something she didn't want. I took her over the outdoor course, and she loved those jumps. I think you have a good eventer on your hands."

"Really? Great. I have Petey, but he's injury-prone. It's been hard to keep him sound the entire season." A voice murmured in the background. "Shit. I've got to go. Have to ride in a jumping class."

"No problem. Call me later tonight and we'll see about getting you back here for a couple of days to try her out before we ship her back to your place." He paused for a second, then blurted, "I love you, Austin."

He hung up before Austin could respond. He knew he'd hear about that tonight when Austin called him, but he couldn't stop what his heart wanted to say. He did love Austin. They had spent three months together, living in the same house and sleeping in the same bed. He'd learned so much about Austin during that time and he'd grown to love the man.

Branimir let his feet drop to the floor and rested his elbows on his knees, staring at the picture of Til he had on his desk.

"I wish I could talk to you one last time. I don't think you'd be angry with me for falling in love with Austin. Actually, I think you'd like him. He's a lot like you, but different. I'm not replacing you with someone else. There's room in my heart to keep loving you and opening it up to Austin."

He swallowed and cracked his knuckles.

"I'm not taking your pictures down, but maybe it's time to start putting new ones up. Austin isn't going to be jealous about my relationship with you. Well, as long as I don't compare him to you."

A knock interrupted his one-sided conversation. He pushed to his feet and went to open the door. Lissa stood on the other side, an annoyed expression on her face.

"What do you need, Lissa? I still have a few minutes before the next class starts." He double-checked his watch to make sure he was right.

"I know, boss, but there's some guy here who says he needs to talk to you right away. He keeps insisting he's your brother."

"Tell him to make an appointment. I don't have any time today. Too many lessons and I have a potential buyer coming around two." Branimir paused as he processed what she'd said. "My brother?"

"Yes, sir. I told him all that, but he won't take no for an answer. He says it's really important for him to see you. I didn't know you had a brother."

Branimir growled low in his throat. If it were true, why would one of his brothers show up at his farm? "I'll go and talk to him. Can you start bringing the horses in for the kids? They should start arriving soon."

"Yes, sir."

He started to walk toward the front of the barn. He stopped and turned back to her. "Did you get his name?"

Branimir's heart skipped a beat. Which one of his brothers had chosen to show up at this point in time? Guess he should've been happy no one had showed up before this. His father might have kicked him out of the herd, but they still expected him to contribute to the ranch, which he hadn't been doing since he moved to Kentucky.

"You know what...I'm just going to need you to take over my class, Lissa. It totally sucks and I'm sorry about it, but I need to deal with this. You can take off early if you want. I'll cover your later classes."

"Works for me, boss. He's out by the first paddock. I wouldn't let him in the barn."

Lissa was very protective of the horses, and she knew they didn't like strangers. Branimir didn't like the idea of his horses being in contact with his brother. Most shifters considered themselves superior to their natural brethren. His family tended to be one of those, except for Branimir.

He headed out and paused for a second in the shadows of the barn, staring out at the man standing next to the fence. One of his retired racehorses allowed his brother to pet her. At the sight of the cast on the man's arm, he moved forward.

The sound of his footsteps on the gravel walk caused the man to turn. He gasped as the sight of bruises and cuts greeted him. His younger brother, Drahomir, grimaced.

"Yeah, I know. It doesn't look good, but I can say it looks worse than it is." Drahomir held up his arm. "Well, except for this."

"What the hell happened?"

Even as he asked, Branimir knew what had caused Drahomir's injuries.

"Father happened. Guess I got too big for my britches or something. He finally kicked me off the ranch." Drahomir shrugged. "I wasn't surprised when it happened. Well, I guess the fact he beat my ass did shock me. He could've just asked me to leave and I would have. Hell, I was ready to leave anyway."

Branimir didn't try to hug his brother, figuring he was covered with bruises. "Come with me up to the house. You can stay here for a few days until you figure out what you want to do."

"Yeah, about that..." Drahomir scuffed his boot along the ground. "I already had my bus ticket for Kentucky before Father decided to show me the door. He never told us why you left, and I just found out he'd known where you were all along."

"Sorry, but I had to get out of there before Father killed me." Branimir untucked his shirt and lifted the hem so Drahomir could see the scar their father had given him.

Drahomir's eyes widened. "Holy shit. It looks like he took a chunk out of you."

"He tried, but I got away from him before he could do anything else to me. I know why he did it. A dominant stallion doesn't want any younger males around to challenge him. It didn't matter to him I was gay and wouldn't be interested in any of the females."

Branimir winced, wishing he hadn't said that last part. As far as he knew, none of his family had realized why he'd never sniffed around the females on the ranch. Drahomir nodded.

"I figured you were gay when I saw a picture of you and Tilman Harlan at a horse show. You looked really friendly." Drahomir dipped his head, with a blush coloring his cheeks. "It was the picture of you two that made me decide to come here."

"Are you saying?"

"Yep. I'm gay as well. I managed to stay under the radar for a while, but I think they were all getting suspicious when I didn't try to mate with any of the females." Drahomir shuddered.

Branimir sighed. "Where are your bags?"

Drahomir gestured toward the end of the driveway. "I left them at the beginning of your drive. Just in case you didn't want me here. I didn't want to have to carry them any farther than I needed to."

"Okay. Why don't you head up to the house? I'll grab your bags."

Drahomir paused and looked over at the outdoor arena, where the first lessons of the afternoon were starting. "I don't want to take you away from your job. I could sit on the front porch until you're ready to quit for the night."

Branimir shook his head. "Lissa's covering for me until later. I'll get you settled in and we can talk this evening when I'm done for the day."

"Is all this yours?" Drahomir waved his unbroken hand at the buildings and land.

Pausing for a second, Branimir took in the well-kept grounds and buildings. He smiled as pride welled in him. The horses grazed on the pretty bluegrass making up the paddocks.

"Yes, this is all mine. Til and I started it about fifteen years ago, shortly after we met out in Montana. Most of the land was Til's, but we added more land over the years." He sighed. "Til's been gone five years now. So I've been doing most of it on my own since then."

"I'll be willing to help out. I can still do stuff, even with a broken arm. I don't expect you to take me in without me paying for it." Drahomir seemed earnest about it.

"We'll see tomorrow after you've rested. It's a long trip from Montana and you've been injured." Branimir held up his hand to stop Drahomir from saying anything else. "Don't worry. I'll put you to work. The horses here are special to me. I don't want you treating them like they're lesser than us."

His younger brother nodded. "Don't worry about that. I'm not like Father and the rest. I admire the non-shifters. In some ways, I think their lives are much less complicated than ours."

Branimir chuckled. What he said was the truth. Dealing with the human side of his personality was hard enough without having to mingle the animal side into it. He gripped Drahomir's shoulder.

"Go on up. I'll grab your stuff and be up there in a minute."

*   *   *

Austin shut his hotel door and leaned against it, rubbing his temples. He'd forgotten how tiring shows could be. Usually, he didn't mind the bustling and visiting people he only saw at shows, but after the conversation with Branimir, he wanted to find a quiet place to call his lover back.

He pushed away from the entrance and started stripping as he wandered across the room to the bathroom. After turning the shower on, Austin went to dig out a bottle of Tylenol for his headache. He swallowed two of them and, before he climbed under the water, he ordered some food from room service.

Rinsing the day's grime off, he hummed under his breath. The only thing to make the shower better would have been Branimir in there with him, but Austin knew why Branimir stayed at the farm.

Had Branimir really told him he loved him? And then hung up on him like Branimir had been just as shocked as Austin at the words he'd said. Austin's afternoon was filled with classes and meetings, so he couldn't call Branimir back, asking him what the hell the man had meant by saying he loved him.

What a day it had been. He'd ridden in ten classes, cutting a couple of them close enough his grooms needed to bring his mounts to the gates. He'd managed to keep the phone call at the back of his mind, so it didn't mess with his riding. He placed in six classes, and while it would have been nice to place in the other four, at least his horses made a good showing.

He dried off and slid on some sweats and a T-shirt he'd stolen from Branimir. It had stopped smelling like him a few days ago, but Austin liked to wear it, knowing it used to belong to Branimir. He dug his phone out of the pocket of his jeans on the floor.

Austin flopped back on the bed, holding his phone in his hand while he stared up at the ceiling. Should he call Branimir now or wait until the food arrived?

He must have dozed off while trying to make the decision because knocking on the door woke him up. He stumbled to his feet and staggered to the door, yanking it open before the bellhop could knock again. He signed the charge slip and stood aside to let the man wheel the cart in.

Austin studied the food for a moment before deciding he wanted to talk to Branimir first. He grabbed his phone from where it'd fallen on the floor when he fell asleep. After hitting speed dial, he leaned back against the pillows and waited.

"Hello?"

He frowned. Who was answering Branimir's phone?

"Hello, this is Austin Spellsin. May I talk to Branimir, please?"

"Oh, sure. Hey, Bran, an Austin Spellsin wants to talk to you," the strange voice yelled in Austin's ear.

"Drahomir, why are you answering my cell phone? You know better than that."

Austin heard Branimir admonish whoever Drahomir was.

"I know, but you were busy and it kept ringing. I can't let a phone ring without answering it. It's not like I spilled the family secret or anything like that." Drahomir sounded young.

"Damn it. Shut up and go to bed. You have to get up early to help with the horses tomorrow." Branimir must have grabbed the phone from Drahomir. "Hey, Austin, sorry about that."

"Who's Drahomir and what family secret didn't he spill?" he couldn't resist asking.

Branimir chuckled. "Drahomir is my younger brother, who showed up unexpectedly on my doorstep today. He got into a little trouble at home and decided I was a safer bet than our father."

Austin frowned. "Is your father that bad?"

"You have no idea. Anyway, he's going to be staying with me for a while. He can't do much at the moment since his arm's broken, but he can do a little bit of work." Branimir cleared his throat. "How did your afternoon classes go?"

"Fine, with no help from you. What the hell were you thinking? First you tell me you're my boyfriend and then you blurt out you love me. After shocking me like that, you hang up on me without giving me a chance to reply."

"Yeah, I panicked."

"You panicked?" Austin shook his head. "Were you not planning on telling me you loved me?"

Branimir snorted. "Not really. It wasn't very romantic or anything.

65

At least, we should have been in the same room when I spilled my guts, so we could have wild monkey sex afterward."

Austin shook his head. "Wild monkey sex?"

"Isn't that what people usually do after they declare their love for each other?"

An evil thought jumped into Austin's mind. "Maybe when both people declare themselves, but I don't recall ever saying I love you back."

During the pregnant pause, Austin could hear Branimir breathing. He didn't let the man stew for long.

"I do love you, Branimir, and next time I see you, I'll make sure I have the night totally free, so we can spend all of it in a bed."

Branimir's relief was palpable. "You bastard. That wasn't very nice."

"No, it wasn't, but I couldn't help it. What family secrets are you hiding from me, Branimir? Any skeletons in the closet I should know about before I hitch my wagon to your star?"

The silence swelled between them again, and Austin started to worry. While he didn't think Branimir was lying to him about loving him and all that other shit, he'd had the feeling for a while now that Branimir was lying to him about something. And that something seemed to be connected to his family.

"There aren't any secrets, honey. There's nothing strange about my family at all."

"Except your father has a habit of running his sons off his ranch," Austin pointed out.

"Well, most fathers want their sons to be able to take care of themselves. It's just his way of making sure we can." Branimir didn't sound any more convinced by that statement than Austin did.

"Mine told me I had to make my stables turn a profit in three years or he was shutting me down." Austin laughed. "My dad wouldn't lay a hand on me."

"I guess my father's just an old-fashioned kind of guy."

Branimir fell silent, and Austin tried to decide if he should continue the line of questions or let it slide for now. He chose to let it go. When he had time and they were face-to-face, he'd talk about the secrets he knew Branimir hid from him.

"So what did you want to talk about when you called earlier?"

"Oh, I wanted to see when you could come back to the farm and ride Mary's Gospel. She's ready to go. I just want to see the two of you together to make sure it's the right fit for both of you." Branimir paused, and Austin could almost feel him thinking. "Or I could trailer her up to your barns. With Drahomir here, I can be away from the place a little longer than usual."

"Your brother is as good with horses as you are?" Austin sat up and grabbed his fork. He'd eat while they talked. Branimir wouldn't mind the lack of manners that implied.

"It runs in the family."

"Hmmm...why am I not surprised?" He took a bite of his steak, chewed and swallowed before saying, "I think, with the current show schedule, it'd be easier if you brought Mary up to my barns. Bring Sparky along as well. Mary likes him and, like you said, I can use him for riding lessons."

Branimir whistled. "I knew you'd see it my way. I'll bring Sparky and I'll give you a good deal on him."

"Really? Do I get like a boyfriend discount or something like that?" he teased.

"Not necessarily a boyfriend discount, but a retired Thoroughbred wouldn't cost that much to begin with. Just give me money to cover the gas for the trip up to your place and I'll call it good."

Austin agreed to it, but he was already planning to donate money to Branimir's rehab center. Also, he would be talking to his family about who should receive the company's annual charitable donation. Together, they would cover a lot of Branimir's expenses.

"I don't expect you to let me off the cost of Mary's re-training. You'll be bringing a bill with you for that."

"Sure. When will you be home next?"

"A week from today. I'd planned on calling you and seeing if you'd be available for a visitor, but this way you can come and check out my facilities. I hope you're as impressed with mine as I was with yours."

Branimir's voice lowered. "Oh, I was very impressed with yours. In fact, I miss yours, especially at night when I'm by myself."

Austin pushed the food away and fell back on the bed, sliding his hand down his stomach and under his sweats. He fisted his cock and pumped.

"What do you miss the most?"

Branimir grunted like he was getting comfortable. "I like the noises you make while I fuck you. The way you bite your bottom lip when you don't want me to hear you moan."

Austin let go of his bottom lip and moaned softly as he stroked faster.

"I miss how your tight ass feels wrapped around my cock. How hot you are and the feel of your skin rasping against mine as I ream you. I close my eyes and see how beautiful you are with your blond hair stuck to your forehead from sweat as you ride me."

"Uh," Austin gasped out, not having the mental capacity to speak as he continued to jerk off.

Branimir deepened his voice and lowered it to a whisper. "I love the smell of your cum when you spill it over our stomachs. I like the salty taste of it when you come in my mouth."

"Shit!" Austin cried out as he came, coating his hand and stomach with his own seed.

"Are you okay?" Branimir sounded smug.

"Yeah. I'll be all right. Just need to take another shower and change my clothes, but I can't do that until I regain my strength." Austin closed his eyes and breathed deeply. "Tell me about your day while I regroup."

Branimir returned to his normal voice and recounted his day of training horses and people to trust each other. He spoke of little children coming to their first lesson with wide-eyed excitement. His voice softened as he talked about the handicapped classes he taught so they could get a different kind of physical therapy. Austin's mind came back long enough for him to ask some more questions about that aspect of Branimir's farm.

"It's one of the ways my retirees get to be active without stressing them with too much exercise. Also, the people who come for those classes get to experience a freedom they might not have otherwise. People confined to wheelchairs can move around a ring like everyone else. Those who might not be able to walk without crutches can suddenly be as normal as anyone else who rides a horse."

Austin smiled at the pride in Branimir's voice as he spoke about his students.

"It's not just the ones who are physically handicapped. We have a few who have personality problems or mental issues, but being around horses that never judge you and only want you to love them seems to ease those with mental illnesses." Branimir sighed. "I've seen so much good come out of those classes, and the funny thing is it's not just the humans who derive joy from them. I've seen horses who were depressed or detached from their surroundings blossom when paired up with one of those students. The horses know when someone needs their help and they give it freely without question."

"I love you." Austin hadn't planned to blurt it out quite like that, but he couldn't help saying how he felt.

"I love you, too, Austin, but I should let you go. You've got to be tired from the show today. Call me tomorrow night when you're done."

"I will. 'Bye."

He hung up and stumbled to the bathroom to clean up again. Afterward, he picked up the empty plates and set them in the hallway. He curled up in bed and fell asleep to the memory of Branimir's voice echoing in his head.

CHAPTER 7

Branimir whistled low as he pulled between two large stone pillars and drove up a long gravel drive. Well, the appearance of wealth was rather impressive, and Branimir understood why Austin would do that. Clients needed to have confidence in the man they trusted with their very expensive horses. While Austin might be a great trainer and rider, if his barns were rundown and fences peeling paint, clients couldn't justify spending the large fees Austin charged them.

He coasted to a stop beside another truck and trailer. He turned the vehicle off and stepped out, stretching his back while looking around. People came and went from the different barns and riding rings. Going around to the side of the trailer, he looked in the open window.

"We're here, guys."

Sparky snorted, and Mary tossed her head.

"I know you both want out, but I have to find Austin and find out where you need to go."

"Mr. Javlosk?"

Branimir turned to face the feminine voice. He smiled at the tall, aristocratic looking woman standing in front of him. She didn't return his smile, but he got the feeling it was because she didn't smile often, not because she didn't like him.

"Yes."

"Mr. Spellsin told me to show you where the new horses needed to go. We have them in a smaller barn closer to the main house. He wishes to be able to keep an eye on Mary's Gospel."

"All right. Do we want to drive there or can we walk the horses? They've been in the trailer for several hours now and I'd like them to stretch their legs."

She thought for a moment before nodding. "We can lead them. I'll take the gelding since I know the mare might have problems with strangers."

"Yeah, but Mary'll be fine after a day or two."

Branimir opened the back of the trailer and slid in to clip lead ropes to both halters. He backed Sparky out first. The gelding showed what an old hand at traveling he was by backing out without any problem. Branimir handed the rope to the lady and went in for Mary.

The mare tossed her head nervously. New sounds and scents filled her head and she wasn't sure about the whole thing. He spoke to her, reassuring her everything was okay and no one would hurt her here. Mary nuzzled the front of his shirt, and Branimir used some of his power to connect with her.

He didn't like doing it that way. It was a form of cheating as far as he was concerned, but sometimes it worked out best. She relaxed as he eased her mind about the place, letting her see, as the herd stallion, he was fine with the place and the people.

When she was ready, he backed her out. She didn't panic or fight him, just walked off like she'd been doing it forever. They circled around, letting her stretch her muscles after standing in one spot for so long.

"I'm Branimir Javlosk," he introduced himself to the woman.

"I'm Maria Andel. I've heard about the work you're doing, Mr. Javlosk, and I'm impressed."

Branimir's eyebrows shot up in surprise. Maria Andel was one of the premiere riders on the Grand Prix jumping circuit. She often ranked in the top three for Rider of the Year and to hear her say she was impressed with what he did was a huge compliment.

"Thank you. I'm just trying to make up to them for what other humans have done."

"And more people should do it, in my opinion. But unfortunately, it's not the lucrative investment most people are looking for, so they turn to other ways to make money." Maria looked disgusted. "I told Austin I'd like to come to your facility and see if there were any horses I might want."

Branimir smiled. "You know, I think I have a couple horses that would work with you. Whenever you'd like to come and visit, I'll make sure they're ready for you. There are three who'd be ready to go out on the circuit with you right now. There are a couple that need a little more work, but they could do for you as well."

"Great. If you'll follow me."

Maria led the way over the trails to where a small white barn stood. There wasn't as much activity around it, and Mary relaxed even more. Branimir grinned to himself. Just like any professional horse person, Austin understood Mary would need quiet to adjust to her new surroundings. Keeping Sparky with her would help as well.

"We can let them out in their paddock and I'll show you their barn."

They did, and Branimir hung the rope over his shoulder while they went into the barn. There were five stalls and two of them were occupied. He peered over the side of one stall into the deep brown eyes of a Shetland pony.

"A pony?"

"Austin acquired him two days ago. I believe it has to do with his new riding program he wants to set up. All the horses that are part of it will be housed here, except for Mary. Once she's ready, she'll be moved into the eventers' barn. I'm not sure if Sparky will go with her or will remain here. I guess it'll depend on how she does on her own." Maria patted the pony before moving to the other stall. "This is another rescue. Austin will want you to look at both of them to make sure they'll be okay for beginning riders."

Branimir met the eyes of the stocky grey Quarter Horse. There was a calm curiosity in those brown pools, and Branimir had no doubt the mare would be a good teacher. He'd ride her once or twice while he was here to make sure, but he doubted she had a tricky bone in her body. He wasn't sure about the pony, though the little gelding didn't seem malicious. All ponies tended to be stubborn and difficult at times. He enjoyed working with them.

"I see Maria's giving you the tour."

He whirled around to watch Austin stride toward him. He wasn't sure what they should do. Did Austin like public displays of affection? Or would he prefer a business-like handshake?

His answer came when Austin swept him up in a tight embrace and kissed him like he was the sweetest piece of Austin's favorite candy. He opened his mouth and Austin's tongue invaded. Branimir's knees weakened as his cock stiffened. *Christ!*

Branimir got lost in the taste and feel of Austin's lips on his. He forgot where he was and who might see them. All he could think about was how good it felt to have Austin in his arms again.

A discreet cough broke them apart. He blushed when he saw Maria staring at them with a rather amused expression. Branimir coughed, but Austin grinned at her and winked.

"Sorry, Maria. Haven't seen him in a while. Can't blame a guy for being eager to get a little sugar from his boyfriend."

"Of course not, but considering how many people are around outside, you might consider taking it somewhere more private." She smirked at them.

"Oh, right." Austin chuckled as he turned to look at Branimir. "Can I see her?"

Branimir nodded. "This is your place, and she's your horse. From now on, I'm just an interested by-stander."

"Yeah, right."

Austin started to stroll toward the paddock where Mary and Sparky were. Branimir turned to Maria.

"Thank you for helping me unload them."

"You're welcome. I'm sure I'll be seeing you again, especially if you're going to be staying with Austin this weekend."

They shook hands, and Maria headed back to the main barns, while Branimir went in search of Austin. He found his boyfriend leaning on the fence, murmuring to Mary, who stood with her nose buried in Austin's shirt.

"Do you usually carry treats in your front pocket?" Austin didn't glance at Branimir as he joined him at the fence.

"Yes." Branimir held out a hand to Sparky when the gelding came up. He brushed his hand over the dark coat and soaked up the warm horse scent. He dug a piece of carrot out of his pocket and handed it over to Austin. "Don't you give your horses treats?"

"Not usually while they're out in the paddocks. They get a little extra something in their feed every night. Keeps them from doing this to riders." Austin gestured to the wet spot on his shirt.

Branimir snickered. "What's wrong with that? You're not doing a fashion show, man. You work with horses, you get dirty. There's no way around that. Besides, it helps the horses get used to me and they start watching out for me to come and give them a treat."

Austin kept petting Mary and fed her the carrot.

"It also helps make the nervous ones less wary of me."

"I can see that, I guess. Do you think I could ride her? Or should I wait until tomorrow? Give her a chance to calm down after the trailer ride."

Shrugging, Branimir said, "As long as you just let her stretch her legs and don't ask too much of her, I think she'll be fine. She's going to have to deal with being trailered to shows and having to compete shortly after arriving."

"Great. Did you bring her saddle?"

"Yeah. You bring her in, and I'll go get her stuff." Branimir handed Austin the lead rope and started to walk off. "She should lead fine for you. Just be careful around her ears. Mary's gotten better about letting me touch her there, but she's still pretty nervous about it."

"Gotcha."

Branimir walked away, allowing Austin to deal with Mary as he would. The new relationship between Austin and the mare had to start being built, and while Branimir would be there to support it, he couldn't interfere in it. He wouldn't be there to fix anything if it went wrong after a couple of days. Austin would have to figure out all of Mary's quirks on his own, and Austin wouldn't beat her if she frustrated him.

When he got back to the small barn, Austin had Mary in crossties and was grooming her. Branimir stood in the doorway, watching Austin's muscles flexing under his shirt. Yep, the man was a heart-stopping hunk and Branimir couldn't wait to get him in bed, under or over him. It didn't matter to him. He simply wanted to have Austin as close to him as humanly possible without wearing the same skin.

Great, now he had an erection, making walking a bit of a pain. He grunted and lifted the saddle onto his shoulder as he wandered over to where Mary stood. He lowered it slowly to the floor, not wanting to startle her by dropping it.

Austin looked up with a smile, his gaze dragging up over Branimir's body, lingering a bit at the bulge in his jeans before continuing up to meet Branimir's eyes. He licked his lips, and Branimir bit back a groan.

"I have to admit I might be looking forward to quitting time a little more than I should today."

Reaching out, Branimir brushed his thumb over Austin's bottom lip. "Don't get distracted. Evening will come soon enough."

Austin nipped the pad of Branimir's thumb before stepping back. "You're right. I can't be distracted with such a demanding lady like Mary here. Let's get her saddled up and I can take her out to one of the outdoor rings."

They worked quickly to settle the tack on Mary, making sure nothing pinched her skin or bunched up under the saddle. The mare mouthed her bit, but didn't protest anything they did. After leading her from the barn, Branimir gave Austin a leg up and they headed to an empty ring. Branimir opened the gate and Mary trotted through.

He leaned against the top rail and watched as Austin walked her around the arena, letting her stretch and warm up. He could see Austin's lips move, but the pair was too far away to hear what his lover said. Austin stopped in the middle of the arena and tightened his girth once more. They walked around while Mary got used to Austin's weight and balance, which was different from Branimir's.

When they drew near Branimir, Austin looked up. "Have you tried her paces?"

"I've done a little dressage with her. She's pretty well trained and has great elasticity. She'll need work on some of the more advanced moves, but I think she'll be perfect as an eventer because, while she's good at dressage, she's not great. Yet she has enough flash to get high marks on her moves." Branimir grinned. "I think you picked a good horse, Austin. Once she's got some more experience under her belt, she'll be a four-star level competitor."

Austin sat a little straighter. "Are you sure?"

"I've worked with a lot of horses. Some went on to be nothing more than good afternoon hacks for retirees. Some have gone on to be the top mounts in their discipline. Trust me…once she trusts you completely, Mary will give you everything she has."

Branimir waved Austin away, signaling him to take Mary out and ride her. Resting his chin on his folded hands, Branimir drank in the graceful partnership between Mary and Austin. The longer they worked together, the more seamlessly they would move together. He was happy he would be around to watch it happen.

*   *   *

Austin concentrated on Mary's movements, making sure she listened to him as he asked for each new dressage step. He could see what Branimir meant. Mary's Gospel had great elasticity and propulsion as they crossed the arena. He didn't ask her to perform some of the more intricate movements, not wanting to get her upset her first day there.

Confident she was talented enough to score high in the dressage portion of an eventing competition, he eased her back into a walk, lengthened the reins, and let her cool down. He kicked his feet out of the stirrups and let his mind wander over his schedule to see when he could open some time up to work with Mary and get her slowly up to speed in order to start going to some two-star eventing competitions. They would work up to the three and four stars. Who knew? Maybe some day she would be good enough to go to the Olympics.

While he was thinking, Mary wandered over to where Branimir stood by the fence. She nuzzled his shirt, and he laughed, digging a carrot out of his pocket for her.

"You're spoiling her," Austin commented as he swung off Mary's back. He patted the mare's neck. "You know, I don't usually let them eat with the bit in. It makes the bit a bitch to clean."

Branimir shook his head. "Don't worry, Austin. I won't do it anymore if you don't want me to. I'll wait until it's feeding time before I give her treats."

"I know I sound like a hard ass, but I can't make exceptions for any of the horses. I need them to have discipline as much as my riders do." Austin ducked his head slightly.

After giving Mary one last pat, Branimir reached over and lifted Austin's chin with his knuckle. "I'm not questioning the way you run your barn or deal with your horses, honey. You treat her well, and that's good enough for me. I know you won't abuse her or anything like that. Your place, your rules."

Austin nodded and leaned forward, meeting Branimir over the fence in a quick kiss. They broke apart when Mary nudged him. They laughed, and Austin held the reins as Branimir opened the gate. They took her back to the barn and removed her tack before brushing her out.

Their conversation while they worked was easy and general as they discussed how Austin was doing at the various shows and how his students were doing as well. After letting Mary back into the paddock with Sparky, Austin took Branimir on a tour of the training facility.

Austin tried to see it through Branimir's eyes and he realized it did look a little ostentatious. It was obviously a big money barn, not like Branimir's farm. Not that Branimir didn't have money, but Austin bet the man lived a little closer to the red than Austin did.

The one thing Austin didn't do at his facility was breed horses. He wasn't interested in the time and money it took to raise a foal. He got them when they were ready to be trained for whatever they'd been bred to do, though occasionally he did get one that had no interest in jumping, eventing, or dressage. Usually those he sent on to someone else. Now, with the idea of starting a riding school for younger kids, he would keep some of those to help kids learn to ride.

Branimir was watching a couple of Austin's trainees take their mounts over a short jumping course. The horses weren't having any problem with the jumps, but the riders looked a little hesitant about some of them. Austin wondered what suggestions Branimir would make to help them.

"What do you think is wrong with them?"

Branimir glanced over at him. "For one thing, they're riding horses vastly more experienced than they are, but aren't old enough to have the patience to teach young riders. The riders haven't developed the confidence to trust their mounts yet. I'd put them on horses like Sparky, older horses who still know more than their riders, but aren't inclined to dump them when they do something wrong. These horses aren't as forgiving of mistakes as older horses might be. Also, I'd have them jumping a less complicated course with lower jumps."

Austin agreed and whistled to get the riders' attention. When they looked at him, he waved them over. He told them to go and let Maria know he wanted them to change mounts. He named two of the older horses with more laid-back personalities. He also told them to drop the jumps down a little.

After they left, he looked over at Branimir, who smiled at him.

"What are you grinning at, jackass?" He bumped shoulders with his lover as they turned to head over to the cross-country course.

"Just impressed at how you order everyone around. Also, when I told you what I thought was wrong with them, you already knew and fixed it right away. You didn't let those pairs continue until both the rider and horse was screwed up."

Austin shrugged. "It doesn't make sense to do that. It ruins my reputation as a trainer if I can't see what's wrong and fix it. Plus I knew you'd know what wasn't working with them."

They paused on top of a hill and looked down at the barns sprawling out below them. Branimir encircled Austin's waist and pulled him close.

"You have a pretty nice place here, Austin. You should be proud of what you accomplished."

"Yeah, with Daddy's money," Austin mumbled bitterly.

"Daddy's money will only get you so far. It'll set you up with horses, land, and buildings, but it won't buy you talent or heart. It can't help you win classes and competitions. You have to do that. You're the one who has to work unbelievable hours to get one horse ready for a class." Branimir squeezed him closer. "You've taken what your father gave you and created something so much more than just money. You created horses people want to spend ungodly amounts of money for. All that hard work has made you one of the top trainers in the country, if not the world. There's probably a waiting list of riders who want to pay you to teach them how to ride."

Austin wiggled in embarrassment because Branimir was right. After he'd won his first couple of shows, people started contacting him about him riding their horses, then after a few more wins, people were asking him to train them. Soon he had more asking than he could handle and he had to put them on a list.

"I like the fact my boyfriend is successful. It's very sexy." Branimir turned Austin so they were face-to-face.

When their lips met, Austin discovered it didn't matter how successful he was...as long as Branimir kept kissing him, he was the richest guy in the world.

They broke apart when they heard hoof beats heading their way. The students were returning. While he wasn't ashamed of the fact he was gay or that Branimir was his boyfriend, it wasn't appropriate to be making out where his students could see him. He sighed.

"I have to work with these two." He waved a hand at the returning riders. "You're welcome to watch or you can wander around the barns. If anyone stops you, just tell them who you are. They all knew you were arriving today."

"I think I'll watch you work for a while." Branimir winked.

Austin rolled his eyes, but smiled before he slipped between the rails and strolled to the middle of the arena. He let all thoughts of Branimir disappear from his mind and he focused on the horses and riders in front of him. The beat of the horse's hooves against the dirt as the horse cantered around the arena while his rider eyed the new jumps. The sound of the rider's soft voice when she steadied her mount as they approached the oxer soothed Austin deep inside.

This was the world Austin loved. The power of the horses contained by gentle constraints by their riders were wonderful examples of perfect partnerships. He loved the smell of the horses, sweat, dirt, and the creak of the saddle as the rider moved to counter the horse. He loved to hear the explosion of breath as the horse pushed his body off the ground, and the thud when he returned to the earth after a pure flight over the jump.

He closed his eyes and listened as the second pair started their round. Sometimes when he just listened and didn't watch, he could spot a problem with the horse before it manifested. The horse's gait sounded good, so he looked up to watch the rider take the first jump. He narrowed his gaze when the rider smacked the mare with her whip as they landed. The mare snorted and shook her head, but didn't baulk as they headed for the liverpool – a jump with a small ditch of water below.

Austin knew Shelly, the rider, tended to get nervous at liverpools. She'd told him she had a fear of water, but he'd never seen such a fear act up when a person was riding. Yet she would force her mount to rush the jump, and he could see her tense as they turned to approach it. She tightened her grip on the reins, causing Bella to fight for freedom to move her head and stretch her neck out. They weren't balanced, and Austin cringed, thinking a crash was about to happen.

He should have known better. Bella had been doing this for far longer than Shelly, and she wasn't going to take a jump without being in the perfect take-off spot. Just as they passed the optimal point for jumping, Bella swerved. The mare knew she didn't have the distance or the balance to make it over the liverpool once they were too close.

Austin was moving before Shelly jerked Bella to a halt and smacked her twice with the crop. Bella snorted and bucked slightly, not used to such treatment.

"Shelly, dismount right now," Austin ordered.

The blonde looked shocked, but she did as Austin said. Branimir was at his side before Austin even thought about asking him.

"I'll take Bella over the jump while you talk to Shelly."

"Thank you."

They lowered the stirrups, and Austin gave Branimir a leg up. He touched Shelly's arm, letting her know he wanted her to stay. He watched Branimir circle Bella, making sure the mare wasn't dealing with any issues from the duck out or the smacks. The mare neighed, and Austin watched as her neck rounded and her mouth softened. Yes, Branimir's touch worked on horses as well as men.

As Branimir turned to head Bella toward the jump, Austin turned to look at Shelly.

"Why did I take you off Bella?"

Shelly shrugged. "I don't know. It wasn't my fault she swerved and I could've fallen off."

"The only reason you'd have fallen off was because you weren't balanced on top of her. You were fighting her. Your fear of water is causing problems with your riding. I've heard of horses being afraid of water and having issues with a liverpool, but I've never heard of a rider having them." Austin shook his head. "You use the crop to get a horse's attention if they're acting up or not listening to you. Just one little tap to remind them what they're doing."

He took the crop from her and held it up to her.

"You don't hit them after they've done something you caused. Bella knows what she's doing, so you need to trust her to get you over obstacles you're afraid of. If you can't trust your mount, then you need to figure out why."

Austin pointed to where Branimir circled Bella at the end of the arena. He noticed Branimir had removed the stirrups altogether, and put on a makeshift hackamore made out of a lead rope Branimir carried with him. His lover rode like he was a part of the mare. Branimir glanced over at him, and Austin nodded.

With the simple action of looking at the jump, Branimir got Bella headed in the right direction. There wasn't any awkwardness or unbalanced motion. Branimir rode like he'd glued his ass to Bella's back. No hesitation as they hit the right distance and Bella took flight. The mare tucked her front hooves up under her and there was no question of her clearing the jump.

The pair practically floated to the ground after making it over. There wasn't one wobble from Branimir when Bella's hooves hit the dirt and they galloped on to the next jump.

"That's what riding is supposed to be. Pure poetry. No struggling or fighting between rider and mount. You have to work on your fear. I'm not sure it's just water you're afraid of. I've seen you act the same way with a few of the other jumps." Austin tilted his head and studied Shelly for a few seconds.

The girl ducked her head and frowned. Austin bit his bottom lip before looking over to see Branimir talking with the other student. At least Celia was taken care of for the moment. He had to take the time to talk to Shelly about her problems. He trusted Branimir to give Celia some tips.

"Branimir, can you give Celia some pointers on how to get Rufus over the triple combination without him ducking out before the third fence?"

"Sure."

"Let's go into the office and talk, Shelly. I want to know what's really going on."

He led the way to his office, thinking sometimes being a trainer was like being a therapist for his riders.

CHAPTER 8

Branimir collapsed into the nearest chair, letting his head fall back as he closed his eyes. He heard Austin hit the couch with a thud and he laughed.

"What are you laughing at?"

He opened his eyes and glanced over at his lover. "I should've known this would be a working vacation for me."

Austin winced before shrugging. "Hey, you're good at what you do. I'm going to take advantage of it."

Branimir leered. "You can take advantage of me any time."

Suddenly, Austin leapt to his feet and grabbed Branimir's hand, dragging him out of the chair. "I think a shower is in order for both of us, and because I'm concerned about the planet, I think we should share water."

"Brilliant idea," Branimir agreed, and they dashed upstairs.

"I'll give you a tour of the place after dinner." Austin tugged him down the hallway toward what must have been the master suite. "Just so you know, this is my bedroom."

He got a quick glimpse of a dark comforter on a large bed before he found himself standing in a well-lighted bathroom. The separate shower was definitely big enough for two people, maybe even three or four at a time. Six showerheads ensured the bather was covered from all angles. Austin turned the water on, and Branimir started stripping.

Quickly, their clothes dropped to the floor. Branimir reached out, grabbed Austin, and pulled him into his arms. He swallowed a groan as their bodies met, skin-to-skin, and Branimir realized just how much he'd truly missed Austin. Their lips crashed together, drawing a moan from both of them.

Branimir slid his hands down Austin's back to grab his lover's tight butt. He squeezed, knowing he'd leave bruises, but not caring. His only thought was to get inside Austin, and fuck the man hard and deep.

Breaking the kiss, he panted. "Where's the lube and condoms? I can't wait any longer."

Austin turned him and gave him a gentle push under the water. "I have some under the sink. I'll grab them."

Letting his head fall back, Branimir enjoyed the rush of warm liquid covering him. He ran his hands down over his chest and stomach to fist his cock and give it a pump.

"Oh my God!"

He looked over to see Austin standing just outside the shower stall, lube and condom forgotten in his hand while he stared at Branimir, mouth open and gaze glued to Branimir's erection.

"Like what you see?" Branimir stroked his shaft again with a grin.

"Fuck, yes!"

Austin tossed him the supplies and dropped to his knees in front of Branimir. After letting go, Branimir caught the stuff before it hit him in the face. Austin licked his lips and ran his finger along the vein throbbing the length of Branimir's cock. Branimir shuddered at the touch and shouted when Austin deep throated him.

He leaned back against the cool tiles and slid one of his hands through Austin's blond curls to cup the back of his head. He tightened his grip slightly to get Austin's attention. When Austin's blue eyes looked up at him, he smiled.

"Don't make me come. I want to be inside you when I do."

Austin nodded and went back to work, sucking Branimir's cock with determined glee. The sensation of Austin's tongue lapping at his flared head caused Branimir to rock his hips and shove into Austin's mouth a little farther. Austin didn't protest, just took everything Branimir could give him. The pair got lost in the moment and it wasn't until Branimir's balls drew close to his body that he realized how close to climaxing he was.

He gently pushed Austin away, and his lover protested.

"Why'd you do that?"

Branimir wiggled the bottle and condom at Austin. "Because I want to fuck you, not come in your mouth. We can do that later."

Austin snorted, but grabbed the slick anyway. "Okay. You get suited up, big boy, and I'll lube."

"Christ, Austin, have you been watching porn or something?" Branimir laughed as he tore open the foil packet and rolled the rubber over his erection.

"What if I have?" Austin coated his fingers and reached around to stretch out his hole. "I have to find fun where I can since my boyfriend lives so far away and I'm busy all the time. I'm not going to go out and find someone else to take care of me."

Austin's eyes closed in pleasure as he prepared himself for Branimir. God, Austin looked amazing, and Branimir couldn't believe how sexy it was to watch Austin get ready for him. He would have to get him do that more often.

He jerked when Austin climbed to his feet, turned, and braced his hands against the wall. Branimir grinned as Austin tilted his ass in a clear invitation.

"Ready? Maybe you should've taken a little more time with that," Branimir suggested as he eased up behind Austin.

"No. I'm good. Doesn't matter if there's a little pain to go along with the pleasure. Makes it hotter." Austin winked at him over his shoulder.

"Okay."

Branimir gripped Austin's hip with one hand, while positioning his cock at Austin's opening. With one long, slow push, he seated himself as deep as he could.

"Fuck!" Austin trembled.

"Are you okay?" Branimir smoothed his hand over Austin's broad back.

"Hell, yes, I'm fine. Or I will be once you start moving, man."

Taking the hint, Branimir fucked Austin hard and fast, slamming into him and driving grunts of pleasure from his lover with each thrust in. He'd missed how good fucking Austin felt and how right it seemed to claim him like this. Branimir leaned over, shoving farther in, and he bit the muscle on Austin's shoulder.

"Holy shit!"

Austin clamped around Branimir like a vise and the waves of his climax massaged Branimir's cum from him. Branimir came with a yell, filling the condom with his seed. As their mutual passion slowly died, they dropped to the floor of the shower, holding each other close until their muscles would support them.

Branimir brushed a kiss over Austin's abused skin. "Sorry about that."

"Why? It was the hottest thing I've felt. It's not like you took a chunk out of me. It'll bruise, but I'll be fine." Austin patted his arm. "We should probably get out before we turn into waterlogged prunes."

"Is that even possible? Aren't prunes dried plums or something like that?" Branimir climbed out of the shower and took care of the condom before toweling off.

He'd run three nights in a row at his farm, so he knew he wouldn't have a problem fighting the urge to shift. He'd even taken Drahomir with him and showed him all the trails his younger brother could run without getting caught.

Wandering back into the bedroom, he looked around at the room and saw bits of Austin in the decorations. The king-sized bed had cream-colored sheets covered with a brown down comforter. The walls were painted cream and pictures of Austin and various people hung on them. Branimir assumed they were family members.

Austin finished getting ready for bed and joined him under the covers. He rolled on his side and spooned with Austin, holding the man close to him. He buried his face in Austin's nape, and breathed deeply.

"I'm so glad you were able to get away. It's not the same talking on the phone. My bed was very lonely."

Branimir grunted. "So was mine."

"How's it going with your brother being around? Are you getting along?"

"We're getting along just fine at the moment. He seems to be dealing with getting kicked out pretty well. Of course, he had to know it was coming, considering what our father did to me."

Austin glanced at him over his shoulder. "Why does your dad drive his sons away? You would think owning a ranch would make him want to ensure there are sons to inherit it when he dies."

Branimir considered how much to tell Austin. "It's family tradition for the sons to go out into the world and make their own way. He really doesn't expect us to come back, though maybe someday, one of our other brothers will go."

"How many siblings do you have?"

Branimir counted in his mind, while Austin ran his hands over Branimir's fingers.

"I guess there were twelve of us when I left home, but if there have been any more since then, I wouldn't know, and I didn't ask Drahomir.

It's not important because until my father grows too weak, he'll continue to drive his sons off the land. He doesn't want to relinquish his position in the herd."

"Herd?"

Branimir winced when he realized his slip of the tongue and wondered how he could laugh it off.

"Well, with as many children as there were on the ranch, what else would you call it but a herd?"

"I feel sorry for your mother. It couldn't have been easy on her to have so many children." Austin seemed to accept Branimir's explanation.

"Mothers." He grimaced, but went with a more acceptable explanation. "The ranch is kind of a commune. There are three women my father slept with to get the twelve kids he has."

"Wow. I thought my dad was bad, though at least he doesn't chase us off when we reach a certain age, although he definitely expects us to be able to take care of ourselves. I think he wants to make sure we appreciate what we have."

"Is it working?" Branimir asked.

"Yes, I think it is. I know running the farm has taught me a work ethic I might not have gotten otherwise. I mean, my father could've taken me in at the company and put me in an executive spot right away. Do you know how much resentment that would've caused?" Austin shrugged. "I didn't really want to be part of the family business. There always has to be a black sheep right?"

Branimir agreed. "Yes."

He happened to be one. Most of the horse shifters he knew stayed out West, where it wasn't any big deal for a horse to be running free. But love had a way of changing a man, and Branimir had given up his freedom to follow Til back to Kentucky. He didn't get to shift as often as he used to do, but it didn't matter because he loved Til.

Now he loved Austin, and he had to continue to keep his secret for a while longer. He'd never heard of a shifter telling their non-shifter mate about their abilities. Not that anyone would brag about spilling secrets. It could mean shunning from the community, and there were a lot of shifters who needed the support of others of their kind.

"I like your room," Branimir commented, wanting to get off the topic of family.

"It fits me. I'll give you a tour of the house."

Branimir tightened his grip around Austin and shook his head. "I think we should take a nap first. Then you can take me on a tour of your house, and feed me."

"Sounds like a plan," Austin murmured.

He listened to Austin's breathing deepen, and soon his lover was asleep. Branimir lay there, his eyes closed, but his mind racing. Keeping secrets from the man he loved went against Branimir's personal code, and he'd hated not telling Til. Yet he'd always done what his ancestors had and lived among the humans without showing a glimpse of the real him.

Stroking his fingers along Austin's arm, Branimir considered what would happen if he showed Austin his true nature. Would Austin freak out and leave him? Or would he think he was having a mental breakdown? Branimir knew he would have to shift in front of Austin, but he'd never done it in front of someone before and he wasn't sure if he'd be able to do it.

His phone rang and Branimir crawled out of bed to dig it from his pocket before Austin woke up.

"Yeah?"

"Umm...we have a problem," Drahomir said.

"What are you talking about?" Branimir sat on the floor, resting his back against the bed.

"Seems Father followed me to your place. He's here, causing a scene. Your employees are doing a good job keeping him away from the horses, but I wanted you to know. I think he's finally gone over the edge, Bran. He keeps shouting about us shifting, and he would never say anything if he was thinking clearly."

"Shit!" Branimir pinched the bridge of his nose and thought for a moment. "Have Lissa call the police and have him arrested for trespassing. I'll be home as soon as I can."

"I'm sorry, bro."

"It's not your fault. You had no way of knowing Father wouldn't just let you go. Now go call the cops."

He hung up and sighed.

"Bad news, huh?" Austin rested his hand on Branimir's shoulder.

"Yeah. I'm going to have to head back home."

"Then I'll go with you."

*   *   *

Branimir looked back at Austin and frowned. "Are you sure? I thought you had another show coming up."

Austin thought for a moment before shrugging. "I can send some of my students with the horses. They need to learn how to make decisions without someone holding their hands, and Maria is going to this show, so I can trust her to keep an eye on things."

Branimir looked like he wanted to argue, and Austin leaned over to press his fingers to Branimir's lips.

"No arguing. You're my boyfriend, and your problems are mine. I know if I needed you, you'd be there for me." He gave Branimir a little peck on the mouth, then he flipped the covers off.

After climbing out, he stretched and yawned.

"Do we have time for another quick shower and dinner?"

"I guess. As long as they put Dad in jail, I've got time to get there." Branimir scrubbed his hand over his face and grunted. "I don't know what brought him here. I can't believe he would actually follow Drahomir. He's never showed any interest in any of his children before this."

Austin shrugged. "Maybe something's gone wrong and he wants to fix things with you."

He chuckled at the look Branimir gave him.

"Okay. Having him arrested says you're not in the mood to work things out with him."

"It's been over twenty years since he threw me off the ranch, Austin. There's no way he can fix this, and I'm not sure I want to go back to the way we used to be. I'm happy with my life, especially right now."

Austin gave an unmanly squeak as Branimir swept him up in his arms and whirled him around. He wrapped his arms around Branimir's shoulders, laughing while Branimir danced them into the bathroom.

"I'm glad to hear you're happy now," Austin said as he turned on the water.

"Don't think I'm comparing you two, but I haven't been this happy since Til died."

Austin closed his eyes and gave a mental fist pump. He knew Branimir wouldn't compare him to Til, and really they weren't anything alike to begin with, but it was good to hear he made Branimir happy. Silly to feel that way when Branimir had already told him he loved him, yet Austin loved the validation.

"I love you," he blurted out as he turned to face his lover.

Branimir blinked and smiled. "I love you, too, though I think you might run screaming after you meet my father."

"He can't be any worse than my father."

"I think you'll figure out there isn't anyone else in the world like my dad. At times, he made Charles Manson look like a feeble-minded idiot." Branimir tested the water before easing Austin into the shower. "We should do this quick. I trust Lissa to handle the situation, but I don't want Drahomir to feel like he needs to take charge. Something tells me my father's been abusing his position as the head of the family."

"You think he hurt Drahomir?" Revulsion rolled in Austin's stomach.

"Well, yes, but not the way you're thinking. He's laid hands on Drahomir. My brother's broken arm is proof, yet I don't think it's anything sexual. Trust me—my father isn't interested in any of his children like that." Branimir paused before frowning. "At least he wasn't when I still lived at home."

Branimir grew quiet while they showered, and Austin could have kicked himself for bringing up those thoughts. He wanted to say something, but he couldn't get his mind to think of something while he stared at Branimir, wet and naked.

After they dried off and dressed, Austin led the way downstairs to the kitchen. His housekeeper, Molli, had left dinner warming in the oven. He pulled it out and they ate without saying a word. While Branimir put their bags in the truck, Austin called Maria.

"I have to go back to Branimir's for a few days. I need you to take some of the students to the show next weekend. You know which horses we were going to take, and there's a list of students and the classes they're in."

Maria didn't ask any questions. She simply agreed to help him out, which was why he planned to ask her to become his assistant trainer when he got back from Branimir's.

As soon as he hung up, they climbed in Branimir's truck and headed out. Austin didn't try to break the silence. He got the feeling Branimir was working some stuff out in his head, and he didn't want to interrupt.

About a half-hour into their trip, Branimir sighed and shook his head. "I'm really hoping he never touched any of the girls."

"Would Drahomir know if he did?"

"I'm going to have a talk with him when we get home. I need to know everything that's been going on since I left." Branimir gripped the steering wheel tightly. "If he has bothered my sisters, I'm going to kill him."

"No, you're not. You'll let the police deal with him." Austin rested his hand on Branimir's leg.

Branimir shook his head. "That isn't the way we take care of things in my family, Austin."

"Umm...okay, but I don't want you to go to jail for murder," Austin commented.

"Don't worry. I wouldn't actually kill him, but he would be thrown off the ranch. We don't tolerate things like that anymore."

Austin blinked. "Anymore?"

"We're not animals any longer. We've integrated our personalities and learned to control them. He should know better."

Austin stared at his lover. What was the man babbling about? Maybe all this stress had driven Branimir slightly over the edge.

"Maybe I should drive," he suggested.

"Why?"

"Dude, you're talking like you were animals and have figured out how to live like humans." Austin squeezed Branimir's thigh. "This might've gotten to you. We probably should've slept for a little bit before heading straight back to your place."

Branimir clenched his jaw, and Austin wondered if he made the man angry.

"There are a few things I haven't told you about my family, Austin, and I'll admit I was hoping never to tell you at all. It seems my father has fucked all that up for me."

"You do know it doesn't matter what you tell me. I'll love you, no matter what."

Branimir snorted. "I hope you feel the same way after I spill everything."

Uneasiness surged through Austin and he settled back in his seat, not sure what to say. He had the feeling Branimir's secrets could change his life forever.

He didn't bother Branimir again while they drove. Austin figured his lover had enough on his mind, and Austin needed to think as well. While he meant what he said about Branimir telling him anything and it wouldn't matter, Austin knew there were some things that could shake him. Like murder or stuff like that. Yet he couldn't see Branimir being a killer or anything truly evil.

They only stopped for gas and a bathroom break. After driving for hours, they turned into Branimir's driveway and pulled to a stop in front of his house. As they climbed out, a young man ran from the house. He threw himself at Branimir, and the older man hugged him close.

If Austin hadn't spotted the cast on the guy's arm, he might have let jealousy overwhelm him. The broken arm told Austin he was Drahomir, Branimir's younger brother, and it was apparent the kid was upset. Austin moved closer, but didn't interrupt them.

Drahomir pulled away and wiped at his eyes. "I tried to get him to leave, Bran, but he wouldn't go. He's stronger than me anyway, and he's the herd stallion. I can't fight him."

Herd stallion? Frowning, Austin wondered at the odd way they had of speaking about their family.

"It's okay, Drahomir. Did the police come and get him?"

Drahomir shook his head. "Yes. I guess he's at the police station. What do you think he's saying? He's crazy."

"Yes. Let's go inside. We need to talk about what's been going on since I left." Branimir glanced over at Austin. "Austin love, this is my younger brother, Drahomir. Dra, this is my boyfriend, Austin Spellsin."

"Hello." Austin held out his hand.

"Oh, hello." Drahomir shook his hand carefully, before turning back to Branimir. "You won't let Father touch me, will you?"

"He won't even talk to you if I have my way. Come on."

Branimir herded them toward the house, and Austin let him. The tension was thick in the air. Lissa came out on the porch. She met Branimir's gaze and gave a nod.

"Go check on the horses and you can send the others home. I'm pretty sure classes are done for the day, right?"

"Yep."

"Good. You can leave after you make sure the horses are okay. We'll be fine."

Austin followed the men into the house. Branimir directed Drahomir to the living room and pushed him down on the couch. Austin went into the kitchen, grabbed three bottles of beer, and headed back to the other room. He didn't know if Drahomir was old enough to drink or not, but it looked like the kid could use a beer.

He held out a bottle to Branimir, who took it with a smile. He lifted the other and tilted his head toward Drahomir. Branimir nodded, so Austin removed the cap and handed it to Drahomir.

"Here. You look like you could use one of these."

"Thanks." Drahomir took the bottle and drained half in one drink.

"Take it easy, kid. Don't need you to get drunk yet." Branimir dropped to the couch next to his brother. "Tell me what the hell has been going on at the ranch since I left."

"I was one when you left, so it took a while for me to notice, and to be honest, things weren't bad for a long time. It's only been in the last couple of years that Dad's gotten weird." Drahomir held up his arm as an example. "He would never have hurt me like this."

Branimir snorted. Austin went and sat on the arm of the couch closest to Branimir. He wanted to lend his support if need be. He rested his hand on Branimir's nape, stroking over the skin there. Branimir visibly relaxed after Austin touched him.

"I know what he did to you, Bran. The mothers say after that happened, Dad was careful never to do that again. For some reason, his beast got the best of him that day. I think it scared him enough to keep it in check, but it's getting stronger again, and he doesn't fight it as much anymore."

"Has he ever touched any of the girls?" Branimir's jaw tightened, and Austin could see the fear welling in Branimir's eyes.

"Hell, no. The mothers would beat his ass if he did. They might let him rule the ranch, but when it comes to the girls, they're in charge."

Branimir's shoulders slumped, and Austin tightened his grip slightly on Branimir's nape. One fear relieved, but there was still the issue of Branimir's father showing up at the farm like he did.

"But lately, he's been having trouble with reality. He spends more time out with the horses than with us. I think he's letting the beast take over, and if that happens, there isn't any one to take over the family." Drahomir fell silent.

Austin tried to stay quiet and not interrupt, but his curiosity got the best of him.

"Beast? Herd stallion? What the hell are you all talking about? You have the weirdest ways of describing your family." Austin shook his head.

Both Branimir and Drahomir stiffened, their wild gazes meeting and clashing. Austin had no idea what the brothers were saying to each other, but some sort of communication seemed to be going on between them. Somehow going whiter than he already was, Drahomir stood.

"I'm going to dig out some painkillers. My arm's bothering me and I think I need to spend some time alone."

Austin blinked as Drahomir practically raced from the room. He looked at Branimir and found his lover staring at him like he had no clue what to say to him. Austin pushed Branimir over on the couch and sat next to him. He took Branimir's hand in his.

"You might as well just say it. Like pulling off a bandage. It'll hurt less if you do it quickly."

Branimir snorted. "I'm not sure this will hurt less. You're going to think I'm completely crazy."

"Maybe, but hey, as long as you're not a serial killer, I think I can deal with what you have to tell me."

"I'm a horse shifter and so is my entire family," Branimir blurted out.

Austin blinked. Did he hear him right?

CHAPTER 9

"A horse shifter? Your entire family changes into horses?" Austin repeated, stunned and slightly unnerved.

"Yes." Branimir peered at him.

"Umm…are you a specific breed of horse?" He shook his head. He couldn't believe he'd asked the question.

"No. I think of us as mongrel horses. No specific breed or color."

"How?" Austin shot to his feet and paced. "How is it even possible? Are you some kind of mutant escapees from a government lab facility? Some experiment gone wrong?"

Branimir cringed, and Austin hated the fact he was probably hurting his lover, but really, how was anyone supposed to take the news the man he loved could turn into a horse? At least, he should be given some credit for not screaming and running away like anyone in his or her right mind would.

"As far as I know, my family and ancestors have always been able to do this. I don't think the ability has anything to do with a government experiment."

Standing, Branimir grabbed Austin's hand and dragged him from the house. Austin wanted to demand where his lover was taking him, but he couldn't get his mouth to work again. His thoughts whirled. Well, being able to shift into a horse would explain why Branimir's cock was as large as it was.

Austin snorted, and Branimir stopped to look at him. A laugh burst from Austin's throat and he doubled over, holding his stomach as he howled.

"Oh God," he gasped out.

Branimir glared at him and crossed his arms over his chest, like he would wait forever, or at least until Austin controlled himself. All that did was focus Austin's gaze right on Branimir's crotch, and he eyed the impressive bulge.

"You're fucking hung like a horse," he yelled, pointing at Branimir's groin and falling over to roll on the ground.

Heaving a sigh and staring up at the sky, Branimir curled his lip in disgust. "If you knew how many times I've heard that from men."

"Yeah, but none of them knew exactly how funny it was." Austin flopped around, trying to catch his breath.

"Whatever. Do you want to see what I can do? Or are you just going to have a nervous breakdown right here in my front yard?" Branimir spun on his heel and continued toward the barns.

Austin lay on the grass, staring up at the sky, and contemplated what was happening. The man he loved confessed to being able to change into a horse. In fact, if Austin wanted to, he could watch him do it. All laughter aside, did Austin want to see Branimir make a fool of himself? Should he be there when it didn't work, and Branimir needed a shoulder to cry on?

He staggered to his feet and raced after Branimir. They passed the barns and followed a trail, leading into the woods. When they reached a clearing hidden from the road or any prying neighbor, Branimir swung around. He met Austin's eyes, and with a wink, he changed.

There were no flashes of light or screams of pain like in the movies. It was oddly like Branimir was simply shedding one skin and putting on another. As easy as Austin stripping off his clothes. Austin's mouth dropped open as he watched Branimir turn from man to horse.

A beautiful white stallion with splashes of brown on his sides stood in front of Austin. He blinked, rubbed his eyes, and blinked again. Nothing changed. Still a horse, and Austin was still outside, not in his bed sleeping, dreaming about Branimir changing into a horse.

"Well, at least you're a pretty one," he commented, not sure what to say.

What did one say to his lover when said lover was a horse?

"Do you understand me when you're like this?"

Branimir whinnied and nodded.

"Oh great." A sudden thought hit Austin. "Christ, if anyone finds out, I'm going to jail for bestiality."

Snorting loudly, Branimir stomped his front hoof on the ground and tossed his head. Austin had the feeling he annoyed him with his flip comments, but he couldn't help it.

"Give me a break, Branimir. You just changed into a horse right in front of me. Am I supposed to fall all over you and exclaim how beautiful you are?" Austin paused for a second. "Of course, you are quite a gorgeous creature. Looks definitely translate well between the species."

Branimir whirled around and took off, racing from the clearing. There wasn't any way Austin could catch him, plus he wasn't sure he wanted to try at the moment. Too many things raced through his head, and he needed time to adjust to what he'd seen. He wandered back to the barns.

Working with horses kept his hands busy while his mind processed things, and Austin needed to figure out just what he was going to say to Branimir when his lover returned. Maybe he should have let Branimir know he wouldn't abandon him. While having a shifter as a lover, and admittedly, it was a shock to even know they existed, Austin didn't care. As long as Branimir didn't make love to mares, even while he was a stallion, Austin couldn't see being a horse as a problem.

He brought one of the horses out of their stall and hooked her in the crossties. He grabbed her grooming kit and started brushing. The mare looked at him quizzically, but didn't shy away as he made her coat shine.

Was the scar marring Branimir's side from his father? Had his father, as the herd stallion, driven Branimir away, not caring how seriously he injured his son, as long as the threat to his position was gone? Had the same thing happened to Drahomir?

Austin shook his head. He thought his father was rough on his kids, forcing them to make their own way in the world instead of supporting them with his gobs of money, except for enough to start his barn. After that, all the money came from sales or winning shows. At least, his father never physically tried to kill him or his siblings.

As Austin brushed the mare, he thought about what he'd just seen. It was a miracle in a way. To be able to change the very form you were born with...though he didn't know, maybe Branimir had been born a horse that could change into a human. He'd have to ask about that.

He paused in mid-stroke. Being willing to ask questions meant he accepted what Branimir was and did, didn't it? Could he live with a man who shifted into a horse at a whim? Was he truly okay with the whole idea?

Yet nothing really had changed. Branimir wasn't any different now than he was a half-hour ago. So he could shift into a horse. It wasn't like the ability suddenly had appeared and now Branimir would be completely different or weird about it. Austin snorted, and the mare shifted her weight, bumping his hand to remind him of what he was doing.

"Oh, I'm sorry, Your Majesty. Was I not paying you any attention?" He chuckled and began grooming her again.

"Do you hate me now?"

Branimir's soft question startled Austin, but he managed not to jump and scare the horse. He set the brush down and turned to look at Branimir. His lover's shoulders were slumped, and worry colored his expression. Austin found he couldn't let Branimir continue to think he might hate him or fear him.

Austin strolled over to Branimir and wrapped his arms around Branimir's waist. He pulled the man tight to him and kissed him. He poured all his love and lust into their embrace, trying to convince Branimir with actions.

Branimir groaned and opened to him, letting their tongues stroke and tease. Finally, their lungs burned for want of air, and the mare snorted to remind them she still stood in the aisle way. They broke apart, and Austin grinned as Branimir touched his lips with his fingers.

"I hope you know I don't hate you." Austin turned to unsnap the horse. "I'm sorry I laughed at you. My reaction wasn't quite what you were expecting, huh?"

"Yes. I didn't really think the first person I revealed my inner creature to would roll around on the ground, laughing his ass off, and making stupid horse puns." Branimir slid open the mare's stall door and stepped aside as Austin led her inside.

"Umm…yeah, I am sorry about that. I don't really know what came over me, except maybe shock. It isn't every day a man's lover turns into a horse in front of him."

Something Branimir said made Austin stop and replay Branimir's last couple of sentences in his head. Shock rippled through him. He shut the stall door and packed up the mare's grooming kit. He carried it to the tack room without saying anything. Branimir followed close behind him.

He waited until they were outside before he asked the question drumming in his head. He clasped Branimir's hand in his and looked up at his lover.

"I'm the first person you've told about being a horse shifter?"

Branimir nodded.

"You never told Tilman?"

"No. There wasn't any reason to. Maybe when we got older, I would have said something, but I never really thought it was important for Til to know. I managed to keep it a secret. There are trails and clearings in the woods I own where I run." Branimir dropped his gaze to the ground. "Is it terrible of me to say, if my father hadn't shown up here, I probably wouldn't have said anything to you either?"

Austin paused, and even though his first reaction was to say yes, it was terrible for Branimir to admit he'd never tell Austin, he realized he had to see things from Branimir's point of view. It had to have been scary to think the man he loved might turn his back on him, if he couldn't handle the truth.

Also, what would the government and scientists do to Branimir and his family if they found out? They would be taken and experimented on without any say of their own. Austin didn't want that to happen, even if he didn't love Branimir with all his heart.

He squeezed Branimir's hand. "Don't worry. I understand why you wouldn't have said anything. Also, I won't say a word to anyone about this. I don't want you or your family in danger because of something I might say."

Branimir slung his arm over Austin's shoulders and hugged him tight. "Thanks, Austin. I trust you, and that's why I wasn't as freaked out about telling you as I used to be."

They strolled up toward the main house, arm in arm, and Austin thought about how this could be something he could get used to every night. Walking into their home together, after putting the horses to bed. It was something that could happen. It would just take a little re-organizing of their lives to merge them. Would Branimir be interested in doing that?

After entering the house, Branimir locked up the place, and they went to the kitchen. Neither of them seemed interested in going to bed yet. Drahomir sat at the table, staring at the beer bottle in his hands. The young man jumped when they entered and he eyed them cautiously.

"Don't worry. I won't tell." Austin slapped Drahomir on the shoulder as he walked past to get to the refrigerator.

Drahomir spurted. "You told him?"

Branimir met his younger brother's accusing stare with a steady look of his own. "Yes, I did. I didn't see the point of keeping it a secret from him when we'd pretty much spilled the beans earlier. Also, when I go to deal with Father, Austin's going to hear a bunch of stuff as well. Might as well make sure he understands to keep it a secret."

Drahomir dropped his gaze, and Austin realized Branimir had taken his father's place as the dominant stallion. Maybe that was why the man drove Branimir away—because he knew Branimir would grow to be stronger and more dominant than he was.

Austin shuddered at the thought of how dominant Branimir could be.

$$* \qquad * \qquad *$$

Branimir glanced over at Austin when he saw the man shiver. What was going on in his man's head? He'd discuss it with him later, after he talked to Drahomir.

"Do you want a beer?" Austin asked him.

"Yeah."

Branimir sat down across the table from his younger brother. Drahomir met his gaze through his eyelashes.

"I'm sorry," Drahomir said softly.

"It's okay, but don't question my actions again. I make my own decisions. Father drove me from the herd, and I don't need his permission to tell anyone about us." He looked up at Austin when his lover set the bottle in front of him. "Besides, Father is busy spilling the beans while he's in jail."

"No one's going to believe him," Austin said. "They'll all think he's crazy, and tomorrow, you'll go in and re-enforce what they believe. As long as you act like your father's crazy, the police won't say a word."

Austin sat next to Branimir and grinned, as Branimir and Drahomir stared at him in surprise.

"What? It's not like I do it all the time. It just makes sense." Austin chuckled. "Of course, I do have a rather evil mind. So remember that if you ever decide to leave me."

Austin bumped his shoulder against Branimir's and winked. Branimir rolled his eyes, but turned to face Drahomir again.

"I've established my own territory here, Drahomir, and if you chose to stay with me, you have to realize I'm the dominant stallion here. I won't be a tyrant like Father and I'll listen to what you have to say, but never question me in front of someone." Branimir growled at his younger brother.

He closed his eyes and breathed. He'd never talked to anyone like that, and he had to control the need to force Drahomir to submit to him. He wouldn't be like his father. He wouldn't rule his herd with an iron fist, and he certainly wouldn't keep any the women for himself. He shot a look over at Austin and smiled. The only person he'd keep as his own was Austin. He wouldn't be willing to share his lover with anyone. Not that Austin would be into that sort of thing either.

"I'm sorry, Drahomir. I didn't mean to order you around. Once you get a little older, you'll understand what I mean."

Though some inner instinct told Branimir his brother wouldn't ever challenge him for herd stallion position.

"It's all right. I know what you're talking about since I've dealt with it from Father for years. To be honest, you aren't nearly as scary as he is. Maybe because you're not insane." Drahomir chuckled.

"Well, that's a good thing. I don't date crazy men." Austin reached out and stroked his fingers over Branimir's hand.

Drahomir snorted. "You picked the wrong family to get involved with then."

"Why do you say that? Have you talked to your mother since you got here? Is that how Father knew to come to my place?" Branimir turned his hand over and entwined his fingers with Austin's.

"I called her yesterday morning and told her where I'd gone. Of course, she knew I was coming out East to find you. I never told her where you lived. I didn't want to take the risk of Father finding you." Drahomir stared back down at the table. "You got out. It probably hurt when he drove you away, but at least you didn't have to deal with him as he's gotten worse."

"I wonder how he found me," Branimir murmured.

"It wasn't like you were hiding out," Austin pointed out. "He could've read newspapers or maybe he saw a TV show where you were featured in. Freeland Creek Farm and Rehab Center is getting national attention for your rescue efforts."

"I know, but I can't imagine Father watching TV or reading newspapers. He's very much an isolationist. He doesn't want the outside world intruding on the compound or corrupting the other members of the herd." Branimir took a sip from his beer. "What did your mother say?"

Drahomir shrugged. "She told me I was banished from the herd, and Father didn't want to see me around the compound ever again. She didn't say anything about him not being there or on his way to find us."

"Maybe she didn't know. I bet your father didn't tell any of the women what he did or where he was going. Seems to me you'll have to ask your father how he figured out where you lived, Branimir." Austin paused for a minute before continuing, "You don't have the same mother?"

"No. Our father has four wives, and each of them had five kids. So we have a big family." Drahomir frowned. "It got so fricking crowded around the compound. I finally started spending most of my time out on the range in horse form. Only way I could have any space to myself."

"Twenty kids? Wow. Though, you know, my father has had four wives. He only had three children, and while he might not get along with his ex-wives, he likes all us kids," Austin said.

"Yeah, well, Father might've married his first wife, my mother, but I doubt he married any of the other three. If he did, he's a bigamist and could get his ass thrown in jail for it, especially if there's been any abuse." Branimir finished his beer and leaned back in his chair, never letting go of Austin's hand.

"I didn't realize you were gay, not for a long time," Drahomir blurted out.

Branimir grinned and yanked on Austin's hand, causing the man to tip over into his lap. Austin laughed while trying to rearrange himself without squashing anything vital on Branimir.

"I always have been, which is why I never understood Father driving me out of the herd, even if it's the dominant stallion's instinct. I wasn't any competition to him for any of the women." Branimir shuddered. "I've never been with a woman, and I certainly wasn't going to sleep with any of the women on the compound."

"Thank God for that," Austin quipped.

"What? You don't like girlie parts?" Branimir grinned over at Drahomir, who laughed.

"Well, girls are very nice to look at, but I don't want to touch anything any of them have." Austin wrinkled his nose.

"Worshipping girls everywhere would burst into tears if they realized they would never have a chance with Austin Spellsin."

Branimir chuckled as Austin tickled him. He wound his arms around Austin, pinning him tight to his chest. Austin squirmed and

101

wiggled, trying to break free, but Branimir was too strong.

"Not fair." Austin pouted, his bottom lip trembling slightly.

Leaning forward, Branimir caught it in his teeth and tugged. Austin moaned low in his throat, and Branimir let go of it to crush their mouths together. Drahomir's exit barely registered in Branimir's mind as he swept his tongue into Austin's mouth and teased.

Austin straddled him, rocking their groins together, and Branimir's eyes rolled in his head as their erections rubbed against each other. Grunting, he slid his hands down Austin's back to grasp Austin's butt and squeeze those two firm globes.

His lover broke their kiss with a gasp and let his head drop back. "Oh."

"I think we need to go upstairs because I really want to be inside you." Branimir nibbled along Austin's jaw.

"Yes. Please," Austin begged.

Branimir surged to his feet, laughing as Austin threw his arms around his shoulders. "Honey, I won't drop you."

"I know. You just surprised me is all." Austin bit his earlobe, and Branimir growled.

"If you're not careful, you'll distract me, and we'll end up running into a wall."

"Oh, hot sex up against a wall. Sounds good to me."

Austin wasn't helping Branimir keep track of where they were. He licked a line up Branimir's neck to his earlobe, where this time, instead of biting it, he sucked on it. Branimir's knees almost buckled and he slammed Austin against the wall next to the stairs.

"Hold on tight," he ordered, letting go with one hand.

He slid his hand around and fumbled with Austin's pants, trying to get them open. Austin didn't help matters by kissing and sucking on every part of Branimir's exposed skin. He shuddered and lost track of what he was doing when Austin shoved his shirt up and bit his nipple.

"Holy shit!" Branimir arched his back, just barely remembering to keep his hold on Austin.

Austin's chuckle was evil. Branimir stepped back, letting Austin's legs drop to the floor.

"Get your pants off now," Branimir demanded before dashing into the first floor bathroom. He dug through the cabinet under the sink. "Where's the lube? There should be some in here."

"What are you doing?" Austin called.

"Looking for slick. I left a bottle down here," Branimir muttered.

"I'm waiting for you." Austin sounded breathless.

"Fuck! Got it."

He grabbed the beat-up bottle and rushed from the bathroom. Branimir skidded to a stop and juggled the lube as he spotted Austin leaning on the wall, one hand wrapped around his cock, and the fingers of his other hand buried in his ass.

It was the most gorgeous sight he'd ever seen. All golden skin-covered muscles and blond hair. Watching Austin stretch himself almost brought Branimir to climax without ever touching himself. He closed his eyes and took a deep breath. When he thought he had control, he opened his eyes to see the same beautiful image.

"Don't come," he commanded.

"You better hurry up then."

"Slick yourself up while I get the rubber on."

Austin looked at him, and Branimir tossed the lube at him. He stripped while Austin squirted some on his fingers, reaching back around when he was done. Branimir got the rubber out of his wallet and tore open the packet. He rolled the condom over his aching shaft before grabbing Austin and spinning him around.

Bracing his hands on the wall, Austin tilted his hips and leered at Branimir over his shoulder. "Are you going to fuck me until I can feel it tomorrow?"

"Of course I am, baby. There's no other way to fuck you."

Branimir picked the lube up off the floor and spilled some into the palm of his hand. He coated his cock, positioned the head at Austin's opening, and thrust in. He didn't hesitate or stop until he was buried balls-deep in Austin.

He shouted as Austin's tight channel gripped his erection in a vise-like hold. Branimir grasped Austin's hips and started reaming the man's ass. Austin cried out as well, his hands scrambling against the wall to try to stabilize himself as Branimir slammed in with each stroke.

"Branimir, please. Harder. Faster." Austin begged with his voice and the undulations of his body.

"Whatever you want."

Branimir spread his legs and really went to town on Austin's ass, riding him with all the power he could muster. Grunts filled the hallway, and Branimir wondered, in a brief moment of lucidity, if Drahomir could hear them upstairs. He didn't care. He wasn't about to let worry about his brother's comfort level stop him from enjoying

Austin.

Austin threw back his head and yelled as his climax hit him. Branimir growled as Austin's muscles clamped down on his cock and milked him, trying to bring him over the edge with him. Cum splattered against the wall and on the floor as Austin came. Branimir continued to thrust, drawing Austin's climax out for as long as he could before he lost control and came himself.

His cum flooded the condom, and he trembled as Austin massaged every last drop out of him. His muscles collapsed and he folded on top of Austin. They slid to the floor, and Austin winced as Branimir's soft cock slid out of him. Branimir brushed a kiss over Austin's shoulder before pushing himself to his feet and stumbling to the bathroom.

He got rid of the rubber and cleaned up. Afterward, he grabbed a washcloth, wet it down and took it back to Austin. His lover murmured something that sounded like a thank you as he washed him. Branimir tossed the washcloth in the laundry basket just down the hall from them.

Branimir bent and picked Austin up in his arms. He carried him up the stairs to Branimir's bedroom, where he laid him on the bed. After doing one more round to check doors and alarms, Branimir climbed under the blankets and snuggled close to Austin. This was one of the things he'd missed most after Til died. Sharing a bed late at night with someone and knowing he would be there in the morning when he woke up.

CHAPTER 10

Austin sauntered into the kitchen and grinned when Drahomir glanced at him and blushed bright red. He patted the younger man's shoulder as he went past him to the coffee pot.

"Sorry about all the noise last night, but your brother and I can't seem to keep our hands off each other."

Drahomir snorted. "Christ, it sounded like you two had a bottle of Viagra between you, and were taking advantage of the four-hour erections."

Austin laughed as he sat at the table across from Drahomir. "Do you have a girlfriend or boyfriend?"

"No." Drahomir dropped his gaze to the glass of milk in front of him. "There was a guy I liked back home, but after Father beat the shit out of me, I figured he wouldn't be interested in a pussy like me."

"No talking like that. You aren't a pussy. You left right after your dad beat you, right? And it was the first time he'd ever touched you?"

Drahomir nodded yes to each question.

"Then I think you're pretty brave. You came across country to see a brother you haven't seen in decades. You had no idea if Branimir was like your father or not," Austin pointed out.

"I couldn't stay there anymore. I figured, what was the worst that could happen here? Branimir wouldn't let me stay? Hell, I was already homeless." Drahomir peered through his eyelashes at Austin. "Maybe I should find my own place, though. If you're going to hang around here all the time, I don't think I'll get any sleep."

"Get some ear plugs," Branimir suggested as he strolled through the back door into the kitchen.

Austin leaned back in his chair and accepted the kiss Branimir gave him. He breathed deeply of the fresh air scent mingled with horse and hay. Also, the underlying musky scent that was purely Branimir. All of Austin's favorite smells together. He shifted in his chair, cock filling to tent his sweats.

Shit! They had made love before Branimir went out to feed the horses. Austin shouldn't be ready for another go-round quite yet. His ass was a little sore from some of their activities last night. He saw the way Branimir had climbed out of bed earlier, so he knew he wasn't the only one feeling it.

"Drahomir, do you want to come into town with us? I have to go to the police station and see about Father." Branimir joined them at the kitchen table with his own cup of coffee.

Drahomir shook his head. "If I can just stay here and help around the stables, I'd rather do that."

Branimir swallowed some of his coffee. "Sure. I need you to call either your mother or one of the other wives. Tell them someone has to come and get him. He can go back to Montana, but we're not taking him."

"No need to call anyone. I'll take him back."

All three of them whirled around and stared at the tall man standing in the doorway. Branimir was on his feet and hugging the man in an instant. Austin stayed seated. He didn't worry that the man might be a former lover of Branimir's or anything like that. Branimir was his, through and through.

Drahomir made a strangled sound in his throat, and Austin looked at him. The expression on Drahomir's face told Austin all he needed to know. This was the man Drahomir had a crush on, and who he thought wouldn't be interested in him because of his father's actions.

"Mirek, what are you doing here? Did the wives send you after Father?" Branimir motioned to the table. "Join us. Would you like some coffee?"

Mirek stalked to the table, his eyes never leaving Drahomir. Oh hell, yeah, there was a lot of interest shining in the blond cowboy's eyes as they stared at Drahomir. Austin thought he might catch fire from the heat flaring between them.

The Montana cowboy broke their flaming stare down and turned to look at Austin. He held out a tanned hand. "I'm Mirek Black. I work for the Javlosks."

"Austin Spellsin. Nice to meet you."

They shook hands, and Mirek sat next to Drahomir. He nodded his thanks when Branimir set the mug in front of him. Branimir joined Austin on his side of the table.

"So did the wives send you out here after Father?" Branimir repeated the question.

"No. I ended up here following this one." Mirek tilted his head in Drahomir's direction.

"Me? Why?" Drahomir sounded shocked that Mirek would come for him.

"I wanted to make sure you were okay. You never came back from the hospital. None of the women would tell me anything, so I checked your laptop. The link to Branimir's website came up in your history, and I figured out you must be headed here. I told your father I was taking some vacation time and left. He must've left right after I did."

"I'm sorry, Branimir. I really didn't think he'd come after me." Drahomir dipped his head in shame.

Before Branimir said anything, Mirek wrapped his hand over the nape of Drahomir's neck and gave a slight squeeze. "It's isn't your fault, Drahomir. You had no idea your father would come all the way here to cause trouble for either of you."

Mirek's statement and touch seemed to soothe Branimir's younger brother. Austin nudged Branimir with his knee and wiggled his eyebrows when Branimir glanced over at him. Branimir rolled his eyes, but grinned.

"You came for Drahomir, but will take my father back to Montana?"

"Right." Mirek barely acknowledged Branimir, his entire focus on Drahomir. "You aren't coming back to Montana, are you?"

Drahomir shook his head. "Aside from you, there's nothing there for me."

Mirek grunted, and Drahomir's face looked like it was on fire after he figured out what he'd said.

"I'm sorry. Why would you want anything to do with me? My family's crazy," Drahomir babbled.

Branimir started to say something, but Austin squeezed his knee and shook his head. Mirek and Drahomir had to work this out without interference from Drahomir's older brother.

Mirek shook Drahomir slightly. "Not want anything to do with you?

I left my job in Montana to track you down after you left without a word."

"I'm sorry," Drahomir squeaked.

"We'll discuss that later." Mirek turned to look at Branimir. "Do you have work for me here?"

Branimir and Drahomir both looked surprised, but Austin had seen the lay of the land from the moment Mirek laid his hand on Drahomir.

"If he doesn't, I could use someone at my place. It's four hours away from here, but since there'll be a lot of business between Branimir and me, I can see someone having to travel between the two places quite often." Austin winked at Drahomir.

"Good enough. I appreciate the offer, Mr. Spellsin." Mirek tipped his head to Austin. "Now you were saying you wanted to head into town to get your father. I'll go with you, and we'll leave the minute the police let him go. I want to get out to Montana, grab my stuff, and get back here as soon as possible."

Austin poked Branimir in the side. His lover turned an irritated glare at him, and Austin pointed at Mirek. "He asked you a question, and you haven't answered him. Also, he's offering to take your father back to Montana. That means you wouldn't have to do it."

Branimir seemed to shake off his shock. "Right. The job is something we can work out when you get back. Whether you work for Austin, or me you'll have a job with us. I appreciate your offer to take my father back. If you think you won't want to kill him after an hour on the road with him, I'll gladly take you up on it."

"I've dealt with your father for over fifteen years. I know what he's like, and as long as I keep the ultimate goal in mind, I won't pitch him out of my moving truck on I-80."

From the way Mirek continued to stroke his fingers along Drahomir's nape, Austin had a pretty good idea what the ultimate goal was. He shot to his feet and grabbed Branimir's arm, dragging him up as well.

"We're going to get ready. We'll be back down in twenty minutes at the most," he told them as he yanked Branimir down the hall toward the stairs.

"What the hell are you doing? I don't need to take a shower or change my clothes," Branimir complained.

"You might not, but those two in there need to talk, and the best way for that to happen is if we aren't in the room with them." Austin entwined his fingers with Branimir's. "Besides, you can keep me company while I take a shower, but you can't get in there with me or it's going to take way longer than twenty minutes for me to get ready."

Branimir settled on the toilet, while Austin stripped and turned on the shower. "I never thought Mirek went our way," Branimir mumbled.

"It doesn't necessarily means he does. He could just like your brother in that way. It happens sometimes. People fall in love with the person, not the person's sex." Austin had seen it with a female couple he knew on the circuit. They both had had boyfriends, but when they met, they fell in love with each other.

"Of course, I never thought about Mirek in a sexual way anyway. He was always just there. I think I was caught up in my own problems, so I didn't really look at anyone on the compound." Branimir sighed.

Austin climbed in under the water and peeked around the curtain. "You aren't going to freak out about them being together, are you?"

Branimir shook his head. "Whatever goes on between them is just that, between them. I don't plan on involving myself in their relationship. They'll have to work things out. Good thing I was thinking of hiring a few new people."

"Well, you have two guys willing to help you, and like I said, Mirek can always come to work with me." Austin soaped up his hands and washed his chest. "I guess I should probably start looking for a facility around here."

"Why?"

Austin paused and frowned. Maybe Branimir didn't want him to move so they could be closer to each other. Talking about it while taking a shower probably wasn't the best place to do it, but he'd started it and he needed to finish it.

"I'd like to be closer to you. That way we can see each other more often."

"Right." Branimir stood and reached around the shower curtain to run his hand over the curve of Austin's ass. "Sorry. All of this has thrown me off. We can stop at the realty agent and get them looking around the area for you. Do you have any idea what you'll need?"

They chatted about what kind of land and room Austin would need to move his entire operation down to Versailles or at least closer than four hours away. He finished his shower, dried off, and got dressed. It was close to the twenty-minute mark when they made their way down stairs.

Mirek and Drahomir were still sitting at the table, but they were closer, and Drahomir's flushed face told Austin something had been worked out between them. Austin winked at Drahomir when he looked up at them. Drahomir stuck out his tongue, and everyone laughed.

"All right. Let's head out. Drahomir, can you rinse out the cups and put them in the dishwasher?"

Drahomir nodded at Branimir's request.

"Great. When you're done with that, head down to the office in the main barn. Lissa will find something you can do. It won't be anything too strenuous. We don't want you making your arm worse." Branimir ruffled Drahomir's hair. "Once it's completely healed, we'll see about getting you riding. I have a bunch of horses who always need some exercise."

"Awesome."

*   *   *

Branimir smiled at his younger brother's enthusiasm. Today, he wished he could have some of it, but he knew the day was just going to get harder from that moment on.

"We need to get going. The sooner I can leave town with your father, the sooner I can get back here," Mirek spoke up from the doorway.

"Yes."

He glanced over at Austin, and his lover nodded at him. Branimir admitted to himself he was still slightly in shock that Mirek had shown up here. The man didn't know anything about their shifting abilities, or at least Branimir didn't think he did. Of course, he'd never really been able to read Mirek. The cowboy came to work for Branimir's father when Mirek was sixteen, around the same age as Branimir. They had been friends of a sort until Branimir left.

Now it appeared there was something going on between Mirek and Drahomir. As much as Branimir would like to warn Mirek about hurting his younger brother, Branimir knew Drahomir wouldn't appreciate Branimir being protective of him.

Austin and Branimir climbed into Branimir's truck. They waved to Drahomir as they left, a beat-up red Ford truck following them. Branimir grew tenser the closer they got to town. It had been close to twenty years since he'd seen his father and he didn't know how he would handle dealing with him now.

Branimir shot Austin a look when Austin reached over and rested his hand on Branimir's thigh.

"Don't worry. I'm here with you, and together we'll deal with whatever your father throws at us."

After taking one hand off the wheel, Branimir clasped Austin's hand and entwined their fingers. He took a deep breath and allowed some of his stress to fade. Austin was right. Together, they could face his father, and hopefully, get the man sent home before he ruined everything. Branimir didn't want to have to leave, though why any sane person would believe a raving old man about changing shapes would surprise him.

"Thanks, Austin. I appreciate you being willing to stand by me." Branimir curled his upper lip. "I know finding out your boyfriend is a horse shifter, then having to deal with his crazy father isn't exactly a couple of normal days for anyone."

Austin laughed. "Don't worry. This is all a little weird, but I've dealt with crazy people before. You've never dealt with parents who spend tons of money on horses too talented for their children, then spend every moment yelling at you for not making their offspring the next Mark Todd or Beezie Madden. They can be far more frightening than some old man rambling on about men turning into horses."

Branimir chuckled, like he knew Austin wanted him to. "I've had a run-in or two with those types of parents, trying to relive their own youth through their children."

Austin started to regale him with some horror stories about a few of his clients, without naming names. Branimir allowed Austin to distract him. There wasn't any point in getting upset until he saw what he had to deal with.

They pulled into a parking spot in front of the police station and climbed out. Mirek parked a few spots down. The three of them joined up at the bottom of the steps, and Branimir straightened his shoulders as he yanked the front door open.

The lady sitting at the desk looked up and smiled at him. "Mr. Javlosk, it's nice to see you again."

"Cynthia, how are you today?" Branimir smiled at her.

"Can't complain." She eyed Austin and Mirek. "Who are these handsome men you have with you? It's rude not to introduce a lady."

"When I see a handsome man, I'll introduce him," he teased. "Actually, this is Austin Spellsin and Mirek Black. Austin is my boyfriend, and Mirek is a new employee."

Cynthia jumped to her feet and raced around the desk, hugging Austin first before squeezing all the air out of Branimir's body.

"Boyfriend? It's about time, honey. Til would never have wanted you to be alone for so long."

"I know."

Cynthia and Til had gone through school together, and been pretty tight throughout high school. Branimir cringed when he thought of how he'd let her friendship slip away.

"Maybe once we get some things settled, you and Frank can come for dinner one night," he suggested.

"Sounds like a plan." Cynthia returned to her seat. "Now what can I help you with?"

"My father was arrested outside my house yesterday for trespassing," Branimir informed her. "I'm here to pick him up and make sure he gets back home safely."

"Oh, right." Cynthia shook her head. "You might want to have a doctor check him out. He's not right in the head."

Branimir sighed. "I know, and it's been something my family has been dealing with for a while now. He somehow managed to travel all the way from Montana. Mirek came to take him back."

"It's sad when their minds start to go," Cynthia murmured as she picked up the phone and dialed. "Hey, Ronald, Branimir Javlosk is here to get his dad. No, he's not going to press charges."

She listened for a moment and then continued, "Right. I'll let him know you both will be right up."

Branimir waited while she hung up and pulled a file off the desk behind her.

"You'll have to sign some papers, saying you're not going to press charges against him."

"I can do that."

As he signed where she pointed, a commotion sounded in the back of the station. He heard yelling and what sounded like people wrestling. Shooting a glance at Austin, he rolled his eyes when Austin met his gaze.

"You have no right to hold me. I didn't do anything wrong. Do you know who I am?"

Branimir cringed as Ronald dragged his father from the cellblock. His father's hair hung in lank strands to his shoulders and a scruffy beard covered his jaw, but even more than that, it was the crazed look in his father's eyes that brought a frown to his face. This encounter wasn't going to go well.

Mirek stepped forward. "I'm here to take you home, Mr. Javlosk."

Branimir's father whirled around so fast, he would have fallen if the police officer weren't holding his arm. Branimir saw the hate in his father's eyes when they landed on Mirek. He lunged for Mirek, catching the officer off guard and yanking himself free. Branimir moved in between them before his father could harm Mirek. He grabbed his father's hand and twisted it up behind his back.

His father fought and struggled, but Branimir was stronger. He worked for a living, while his father did nothing but order others around.

"You'll stop this right now," Branimir ordered under his breath.

His father looked at him and curled his lip in disgust. "So my other faggoty son decides he can order me around. I'm still the herd stallion, boy, and I don't have to take orders from you."

Branimir shook the older man slightly. He felt the fragility of his father's body and didn't really want to hurt the man. "You'll stop talking right now. This is a family matter. Humans can't be involved in this. You understand me?"

All of that was whispered quietly in his father's ear. Something in his tone must have gotten through to the man, or else the determination in Branimir's eyes let his father know he wouldn't allow his father to expose them to humans. The older man nodded, and Branimir handed him off to Mirek.

"Take him outside while I finish up the paperwork."

"Yes, sir." Mirek took a hold of Branimir's father's arm and led the man from the police station.

Branimir turned to face Cynthia and Ronald with a sad expression on his face. "I'm sorry for all the trouble he's probably caused. He hasn't been in his right mind for a while now. I'm not even sure how he managed to get here from Montana without being picked up by the police before this."

Cynthia laid her hand on his arm and squeezed gently. "We understand. He's getting older, and sometimes their minds go. It's hard to watch, but at least you've found him and you can do something about it."

"Don't worry. I'll make sure my mother doesn't have to worry about watching him on her own." He signed the papers she set on the desk and smiled at Cynthia. "I better get Mirek and my father on their way home. My mother's going crazy worrying about him."

"Of course. Give me a call and we'll set up a time for dinner." She kissed him on the cheek and did the same with Austin. "It was nice meeting you, Austin. I look forward to getting to know you."

"Nice meeting you as well, Cynthia." Austin hugged the older lady.

They left the station and went to where Mirek and Branimir's father stood next to Mirek's truck. Branimir stalked up to his father and crowded the man into the side of the vehicle.

"Now listen to me. Mirek is taking you back to Montana and the rest of the herd. You aren't welcome here, and I'll not be going back with you. You made it perfectly clear how you feel about me when you drove me off the compound and away from the herd. No one else stood up for me, so I'm assuming none of the rest of them wanted me there either."

"Well, that isn't true."

Branimir glanced over to Mirek. "What do you mean? And why don't you seem confused about this whole herd thing?"

"Because I'm not stupid. I know what you are, and have known since I arrived at the ranch." Mirek shrugged. "I'm just not a horse shifter."

"Not a horse shifter?" Austin sounded surprised. "If you're not a horse shifter, than what are you?"

"I'm a mountain lion."

"Of course…what else would you be?" Austin muttered as he shook his head.

"Your father was the herd stallion. No one's going to argue with him when he chooses to dive a younger stallion away. It's the law of the herd."

Branimir knew Mirek was right, but he'd always thought they were more evolved than the herd. He sighed. It didn't matter anymore. If his father hadn't driven him away, he would never have met Til and moved to Kentucky. He would never had found Austin after Til's death. In the end, the banishment had worked out for the best.

"It doesn't matter now, even if they did want me back. I have a life and herd here. I'm not going back to Montana." Branimir backed away from his father. "I don't know why you came here, but it's time for you to go home."

"Not without Drahomir." His father puffed up and glared at Branimir.

Taking another step back, Branimir looked at his father, and shock hit him. When had Artur Javlosk gotten old? His stringy, greasy hair was streaked with gray and lines carved valleys in his face. Artur wasn't as tall as Branimir, yet he remembered when his father seemed to tower over him. Artur didn't inspire respect or awe in Branimir anymore, and he realized he was far stronger than his father and could no longer be intimidated by him.

"No. Drahomir stays here." Branimir paused before continuing, "If he wants to, but he doesn't, I'll send him home on his own. He's not going anywhere with you. You've done enough damage."

Mirek growled, drawing everyone's attention. "Drahomir will stay here. We've talked about it, and he knows I'll be returning when I'm done delivering your father to the compound."

Branimir nodded. "Fine. I don't have a problem with Drahomir staying with me as long as he and you want."

"I do. He's my son and he'll do as I say." Artur snarled and lunged for Branimir.

Placing his hand on Artur's chest, Branimir shoved him back and stared at him. "You'll leave Drahomir alone. He's an adult now and can make up his own mind. Mirek, take him back to the herd."

"Yes, sir."

Branimir turned to look at Austin. "Are you ready to go see the Realtor? We should be able to find a place for you close by. Maybe we should look for a house equal distance from both places. Drahomir and Mirek can move into my house at the farm."

Austin's mouth dropped open slightly, but he closed it before launching himself into Branimir's arms for a quick hug. Branimir knew his lover wanted to kiss him, but anything more than a hug would have to wait until they got home.

"Are you sure?" Austin whispered in his ear. "I don't mind moving in with you."

"No. That house was mine and Til's. I think we should have our own house and make our own memories." Branimir hugged Austin tight for a moment before letting him go and stepping back. "Let's get started on creating our own herd."

He held out his hand, and Austin took it. Branimir glanced back once to meet Mirek's gaze. The cowboy nodded, and Branimir understood the look Mirek gave him. He nodded back, silently vowing to keep Drahomir safe until Mirek returned.

"What kind of house do you want?"

Austin's question drew him back to his lover, and Branimir grinned. He had a lover and a life again, and somehow he knew Til wouldn't be upset about it at all. Branimir had one love of his life, and he'd gotten lucky enough to find a second lover who filled his heart as much as Til

115

had.

"We'll figure it out, love. We've got time."
All the time in the world.

EPILOGUE

Austin took a quick peek at the watch on his wrist. They were coming into the last three fences of the cross-country portion of the eventing competition. Mary's Gospel galloped along confidently with no sign of hesitation or tiring. Her ears were pricked forward as she focused on the next fence.

He gathered her energy, steadying her as they approached the huge log jump. Austin knew there was a ditch on the other side and he encouraged her to put more effort into her leap to ensure they cleared both obstacles. Austin rose up in the stirrups, crouching over her neck.

"Steady, Mary," he said loud enough for her to hear him, but not so loud she startled.

One ear swiveled back to catch his voice. Mary came into the jump on the right stride, and she thrust them off the ground with a heave of her muscular hindquarters. Austin remained frozen on her back, not wanting to do anything to unbalance her. The mare must have spotted the ditch as they cleared the log because she stretched out, and somehow they landed clear.

Austin checked his watch again. They were still well within the time limit set for the course. He didn't want any time faults. He and Mary were sitting in third place after the dressage section of the competition, and Austin hoped they could move up since cross-country was clearly Mary's strong suit.

They cleared the last two fences, and Austin leaned forward, giving Mary the signal to give all she could for the last hundred yards. The moment they crossed the finish line and the clock stopped, Austin dismounted. He loosened the girth, and Mary dropped her head.

Branimir met them a few feet beyond the finish line. He threw a blanket over the mare, and they made their way over to the veterinarian's tent. The vets would check Mary out before they finished cooling her down.

Once they got the all clear, Austin and Branimir walked around, wanting Mary's Gospel to cool down entirely before they groomed her and settled her in her stall for the night.

"You had a clean round with no time faults. We'll have to check the two ahead of you, but I think you're at least still in third place. No one else had a time close to yours so far." Branimir squeezed Austin's shoulder and went back to rubbing Mary down.

"We'll check the standings on our way to the hotel. I want to take a shower and a nap before we meet up with the others for dinner." He smiled at his lover. "At least, we're making a good showing for the farm."

Branimir nodded. "That's true, but I don't think we had to worry about our reputation, considering you're one of the best trainers out there."

Austin brushed a kiss over Branimir's cheek. He set Mary's saddle and bridle on the saddle rack in front of her stall. The grooms they'd brought with them to take care of the horses would make sure it was cleaned. Mary was the only horse Austin and Branimir groomed at a show. She still had trust issues and didn't like anyone else near her unless one of them was there.

Branimir made sure there was water and hay for Mary. Austin talked to Lissa about the other horses. Finally, everything was taken care of, and they could leave. Austin leaned back in the passenger seat and sighed. Branimir smiled over at him before putting the truck in drive and pulling out of the parking lot.

"You did a great job today, love. For this being Mary's third competition, I'm impressed you've gotten her so far. I figured we would have a few meltdowns along the way." Branimir got them on the highway and reached over to rest his hand on Austin's thigh.

"I think having you around all the time helped her get used to the rest of us quicker." Austin covered Branimir's hand. "I'm glad we decided I should just move in with you after all."

"Combining our stables wasn't as difficult as I thought it would be," Branimir admitted. "Also, I'm happy you didn't get upset when I suggested it."

Austin shrugged. "We got lucky the farm next to yours went up for sale, so we could expand. Our people work well together. The other good thing is Mirek being back. Drahomir certainly seems happy to have him around."

Branimir nodded. "I hope things work out for them. My brother needs someone to focus on totally, instead of leaning on me. I can't be there for him completely. You're my world now, and he's got to learn to be on his own."

Once they got to the hotel, they took a shower and climbed into bed. As they snuggled close, Austin brushed a kiss over Branimir's chin.

"You know, it's almost like someone's watching over us and smoothing the way for us," he whispered as he closed his eyes.

He was drifting off when he heard Branimir softly say, "Thank you, Tilman."

T. A. Chase

T. A. Chase lives a life without boundaries. Being fascinated by life and how different we all are, she writes about the things that make us unique. She finds beauty in all kinds of love and enjoys sharing those insights. She lives in the Midwest with his partner of fourteen years. When she isn't writing, she's watching movies, reading and living life to the fullest.

*   *   *

**Don't miss *Allergies*
by T. A. Chase,
available at AmberAllure.com!**

What's a shapeshifter to do when the man he desperately wants is allergic to him?

Raymond Marvels never imagines his call to the IT department at his graphics design job would result in his meeting Lou Canis, the most gorgeous man he's ever seen. There's one small problem, though—Ray is allergic to Lou. Yet his allergy is only one of the weird things going on between them.

Lou, a werewolf, isn't sure how to fix the situation, because it seems his would-be lover's allergy is to Lou's human form and not his canine one. Lou decides to tell Ray his deep dark secret, which has unexpected results when Ray embraces both sides of Lou. Yet after a witch doctor gives Ray some medicine to solve his problem, Ray and Lou discover they must also face a dangerous conspiracy evolving around them...

AMBER QUILL PRESS, LLC
THE GOLD STANDARD IN PUBLISHING

QUALITY BOOKS
IN BOTH PRINT AND ELECTRONIC FORMATS

ACTION/ADVENTURE	SUSPENSE/THRILLER
SCIENCE FICTION	DARK FANTASY
MAINSTREAM	ROMANCE
HORROR	EROTICA
FANTASY	GLBT
WESTERN	MYSTERY
PARANORMAL	HISTORICAL
YOUNG ADULT	NON-FICTION

AMBER QUILL PRESS, LLC
http://www.amberquill.com

Made in the USA
San Bernardino, CA
04 October 2013